Your

Lolita

Your
Lolita

D. B. Wells

Livingston Press
at
The University of West Alabama

Library of Congress Control Number 2004093709

Printed on acid-free paper.

Printed in the United States of America by
Publishers Graphics, LLC
Hardcover binding by: Heckman Bindery

Typesetting and page layout: Gina Montarsi
Proofreading: Michael Adair, Beaux Beaudreaux,
Beverly Hise, Joe Taylor
Cover design and layout: Gina Montarsi
Cover photos: Derrick Conner

Some of these stories appeared in slightly different forms
in the following magazines: *New York Stories, Chelsea, Yemassee,
Redbook, Cleveland Magazine, Art Times, New Letters, The Raven Chronicles,
Northwest Florida Review,* and *Peregrine.*

This is a work of fiction.
You know the rest: any resemblance
to persons living or dead is coincidental.

Livingston Press is part of The University of West Alabama,
and thereby has non-profit status.
Donations are tax-deductible:
brothers and sisters, we need 'em.

first edition
6 5 4 3 3 2 1

for Joe Taylor,
thank you.

Table of Contents

Leap

EVERY WOMAN I'VE loved—no matter how big of a bitch she eventually turned out to be—had at least one thing that drove me absolutely crazy. It could be anything. The way she flipped her hair, that split second of butt-bounce after walking stopped, the taste of her most intimate sweat. Each had something different, but the effect on me was always the same: I would be blinded to their awful faults until it was too late and I had married them, or knocked them up, or at least moved their every possession into my place. This is the pattern of my life and I can't change it. Once enthralled, that object of desire begins colonizing my brain cell by cell until I can think of nothing else, until I must possess it and know it with my every sense. Even now, long after I thought I was through the repertoire of feminine snares, I find myself captivated again. And it is this flaw of obsession that led to my recent ejection from the Massieville Endtime Tabernacle and puts me on the banks of this river tonight.

THE LETTER FROM the Immigration and Naturalization Service came one morning when the sky spat sleet at the puddle-pocked parking lot of the Black Jackson Bar and Cultural Center. It was addressed to Duval Vogelpoll and little good has ever come to me from being called that way.
You have been named as the potential sponsor for the Vietnamese national(s) listed below.

A photo was stapled to the page, a mug shot really, showing the jailhouse defiance of one captured but not subdued, the pose of one putting up a tough front in the face of overwhelming force. And she's claiming what? That she's my daughter? Granddaughter maybe. The letter was unclear.

A primer-splotched Silverado splashed into the parking lot. George Goins struggled up the steps, his joints calcified, eyes the color of fox fur, skin the shade of October acorns. A Black Jackson. He stepped behind the bar, tallied his tab and helped himself to a Strohs. I went back to the list I was making:

1.) Get to heaven
    (See the Reverend)
2.) Plan Funeral
    (Waterproof casket)
3.) Cult Center
    (Donate to Univ)
4.) Dogs
    (?)

Johnny Walker stood on his hind legs and hopped in a staggering circle, the little dance ending with his front paws on my thigh, eyes expectant of petting. "You poor dumb sonofabitch," I said, rubbing the massive hinge of his jaw.

"Talkin' to me?" George turned stiffly. "Want me to kick yer ass?"

"Ain't talkin' to you, George. Talkin' to this other dumb sonofabitch."

Johnny Walker was a ninety-pound pitbull with a head like a shovel, the product of decades of close breeding among generations of vicious combatants. But he prefers to dance. Likes to roll over too. Rabbit fawns are delivered wet but unpunctured. And he'll shake hands till the cows come home. I scratched his red brindle chest sending his hind leg into overdrive. What trait of gentleness had I overlooked in his brutal primogenitors? What glimmer of tenderness did I fail to expunge? If Johnny ended up in the pit he'd be killed, would probably try to dance for the audience like he does for the customers of the Cultural Center. So I would have to find a place for him, as well as for Irish Rose the bitch and Jack Daniels the sire, who're both mean as hell. "Pitbull rescue?" I wrote on my list, though I knew such an outfit didn't exist. After I was gone the county would send someone out who would gut shoot the dogs and laugh while they died. That's the kind of degenerate sonofabitch who becomes a dog warden. So I'd shoot them myself, and do it right. But it'd be the last thing I'd do.

George slid off his stool.

"Bring me them Camels, George."

George brought the cigarettes and flipped back the metal cap of his lighter. I liked the soft clank and the low rasp of the strike on flint. I liked the fat flame and the taste of lighter fluid through blended tobacco, Turkish and domestic. I liked the melodic endnote as the worn steel came back together, final and definitive, saying something had been done, a job completed, a cigarette lit.

His quarter fell through the jukebox.

I knew what he would play.

It Wasn't God Who Made Honky-Tonk Angels.

He Stopped Loving Her Today.

Kitty came and got the cash register ready and I showered and combed my beard and sheathed my hair into a tail. I put on clean clothes and my best boots and on the way out the door looked at the photo of the girl again, trying to see something of myself there. Her lips were cracked and chapped like she'd been outside for a long time and her skin was dark as earth, whether from sun or genetic make-up. Whatever her mix, she was quite a concoction. And when the camera snapped, she was obviously scared to death.

I drove through Massieville, past century-old houses made of stones collected from the ruins of the Indian Fort. Past dogs on chains and cars on blocks and the white-washed Methodist Church. Past the general store and the red brick school, Dairy Queen and an oak log cabin slumping back into earth. There were mobile homes that hadn't budged in fifty years, some broken and burned, singed curtains sucked through gaping windows, doors open, pink insulation torn from floor boards by last spring's flood, bright plastic toys and dull rubber tires embedded in brown weeds laid over by snows come and gone. The widow Locklear sat at her window in her wheelchair, withered and brown like a long lost potato just rolled out from under a shelf. I turned into the parking lot of the Endtime Tabernacle and gave a glance to my mother's grave, dug when the church housed Hardshell Baptists. The building was quiet and dark and still held the deathsmell of flood.

"Anybody here?"

A woman with too much hair peeked out of the room beneath the choir loft.

"Chief Vogelpoll?"

"I'm a little early."

"That's just fine. Just come with me."

Mrs. Pugh's skirt fell to the middle of her ropey calves, big as buckets and swishing as her nylons rubbed. The Reverend Pugh stood behind his desk with his hands on the back of his chair, fingers drumming, jowl meat flushed, belt fastened just below his tits. "Well, well," he said, grinning. "Well, well. This *is* a surprise. This is *certainly* a surprise. And I'm glad you came. *Glad* you came. I've been wanting to meet you for years. *Years.* It's long past due." He swallowed some spit. "I'm *sure* we can be friends. I'm *sure* we can be gentlemen."

"Look, I'm not here to raise hell, if that's what you're afraid of. I'm not pissed because you say I do the devil's work."

"You aren't?"

"No. In fact, it's your condemnation that brings me. I could've gotten off easier had I'd gone to the Methodists but I think your opinion of me might be closer to God's. But what do I know? I know nothing about the ways of God. That's why I've come. I'm dying, see, and I don't want to go to hell."

THE BLACK JACKSON bar and Cultural Center is located in the reconstructed Indian Fort, which wasn't built by Indians and wasn't a fort. It was built by a people out of time and out of place. A people embarrassing to the neat arrangement of American history. White people thriving in the American interior when the Puritans were struggling on the coast. The Indian Fort was built by Crypto-Europeans, in the parlance of the few academicians who acknowledged the ruin. The precursors of the Black Jacksons before the infusion of Delaware blood. I bought the site for back taxes when I got out of the army and an archaeologist from U.K. wanted to help rebuild it using sixteenth century technology, but I wanted the thing up fast and used a Ford 555D for the heavy lifting. That's when people started calling me Chief.

There were a dozen cars in front of the Cultural Center when I returned from visiting Reverend Pugh. He said I'd know it when I got saved. He said I'd receive the Holy Ghost and It would take me down like Paul on the Road to Damascus. It would strike me with a blinding blaze and a whirling wind and shake the earth beneath my feet. Until then, he said, I was in the State of Seeking. Not yet saved. But if I availed myself to enough of his preaching, he promised to lay the Lord on so thick that I could not help but succumb to salvation. Until then I had to beseech God without ceasing, confess my sins, and quit selling beer. It was not even noon and the jukebox was already cranked so loud I could feel its beat from inside my truck.

Hoots greeted me when I came through the door. Maybe half the people at the bar were named Jackson. The others were Gipsons, Gibsons, Goins, Gohans, and a Vogelpoll or two. Others were just allied rednecks not directly related to the Blue Eyed Tribe. I stepped behind the bar and turned down the jukebox.

"Can I have your attention please?" I said. "Ladies and Gentlemen, for years now we've been on the road to hell and the time has come to make a course change. Those alcoholic beverages before you now will be the last ever served here. Of course we'll still offer our complete menu for lunch and dinner and occasionally breakfast, and you're all welcome to stop by for coffee or pop, but from now on—"

"To hell with pop!"

"That's right, blaspheme your way to damnation, but when you lift your eyes up in torment, and behold me in the bosom of Abraham—"

"Fuck Abraham!"

"I hope God can forgive that, Alafair. I truly do. I'm going to my room now to ask Him."

Kitty was in the kitchen scooping a fish tail out of the fryer. "Tell me you're not serious."

"I truly am."

"Why are you doing this, Chief? How're you gonna pay me if you stop selling liquor? Who else is gonna pay me when you can't? Why do you have to be so crazy all the time?"

"Those other times you speak of, those other things I've done, were born of drink and marijuana. That's not the case today."

Johnny, Jack, and Rose followed me to my room. I needed to pray, but first I checked in on blackjackson.com. The site had registered six hits since yesterday.

Dear Chief Vogelpoll,

My great-grandfather came to Arizona in 1936 and never spoke of his past. Recently we learned that he was born in 1912 on a farm near Massieville Kentucky....

Another lost lamb outed. I went to Ask Jeeves and typed **how do I pray?** but I should have known better. That sonofbitch doesn't know anything. He only asks you another question. I ended up on my knees beside my bed, the way my mother taught me.

THE FIRST WORDS I remember saying were at my mother's funeral. I was six, so there were other times I had spoken but that is the first time I remember the exact words. There was water in the grave and I wondered what would be done about it. Then the casket was lowered and I knew nothing would be done and that my mother would be wet and that it really didn't matter and that that was what it meant to be dead. It was when nothing mattered anymore. I sat on a folding chair and felt the hands of others on me and, when it was time, I was given a flower and pushed to the edge of the grave. It was then I said it.

"I hate you!"

I don't know why I said it. I sure didn't hate her. I have such little understanding of so many things. Even the things I do.

Johnny Walker came up under my arm and forced his face into mine. Jack Daniels and Irish Rose wagged their tails uncertainly and licked my face. There was a tapping at my door. "You okay?" Kitty asked. "Duval? Are you okay?"

"Yeah," I said, and realized I'd been blubbering.

She was silent for a moment. "Duval? Do you want to talk?"

"I'm fine," I said. "Go on home. I'll lock up."

I listened to the silence of winter. No birds. No leaves rustling. The jukebox was still. There were no voices coming from the bar. No argument. No laughter. The preview of the grave. Nothing. I wondered how I would end. Would Kitty climb into my bed again after all these years? Would she put up with me one more time and hold me as I grew cold? I sat for hours. As the earth turned and the sun left America and rose over the Pacific I sat on the floor trying to pray but feeling my pleas were getting no further than the ceiling, no further than the top of my head. In early morning, a disembodied voice split the silence.

You have mail!

Dear Chief. Tam try to get to you for all time. Tam give name Jackson because of honor to you and attach pitcher for your looks. Tam want america and black jackson. Tam love leap to you from across water.

Nguyen-Jackson Minh Tam

I clicked on the attachment. **Warning! Source unknown. Do you want to save to disk?** I downloaded from the current location and my heart—my actual blood-pumping organ—skipped a beat. A Vietnamese girl sat on the knee of an American soldier. Behind them, the jungle. She was wearing an oversized t-shirt bearing the screaming eagle insignia of the 101ˢᵗ Airborne. The photo was ragged, cracked with creases and dirty. The two seemed to be sitting in a bomb crater, the jungle behind them chewed and splintered by explosion. Yet their youth shined through. Youth and even optimism.

I was that paratrooper. Xuan Lan was the girl, and she'd been dead for thirty years.

I sent a message out of the dark. I sent an e-mail chasing the sun.

NOT MUCH WAS happening at the Tabernacle in the way of redemption in the month of February. Oh, the Gift of Tongues was granted to the same people every week while the Gift of Interpretation was granted to others, the translation always coming out in thees and thous. Sister Heflin could be counted on to have backslid over the week and Brother Cox would give an update on the torment the Lord was putting him through. But for me, the voice of God was silent. So I spent my days slogging through Genesis in my nearly empty bar.

One day, the Collins twins—Wayne and Dwayne—stepped through the door and kicked snow from their boots. Overgrown and overweight, they were in their forties, yet were still boys, their faces unlined by care or worry. They lived with their mother down the hollow with some chickens and a little patch of flat land that grew beans and corn and tobacco for money. They took their usual seats and I knew which was which because years ago, when I'd first opened the Center, they carved their names in the bar and I banned them for life. The letters had been a lighter color than the bar top then. Now, ingrained with the grit of unnumbered drunks, the letters were nearly as dark as the wooly worm cigarette burns that graced the wooden slab from end to end.

"Listen boys, there's no beer because I got religion. Hell is filled with guys like you who drink beer and I'll not be a part of it anymore. See here? I'm reading the Bible."

"We heard yew got a girl."

"That's right," Kitty said. "Chief's got religion and a girl that sits on the floor."

"Kin we see 'er?"

Kitty looked through the service window. "Hey Tam!"

Flip-flop, flip-flop. Not a hundred pounds soaking wet, SOS pad held in her yellow Platex gloves, followed gleefully by Johnny, Jack and Rose. She still wore the electric pink flip-flops and blue pajamas she came in.

"She's blind as a bat, so Chief got her a pair of VA birth-control glasses," Kitty said.

"How they work?" Wayne asked. "The glasses?"

"They make 'er so goddamn ugly no one'll screw 'er."

Coffee sprayed from Dwayne's nose. The girl moved closer to me.

"They're safety glasses is all," I said. "Just a stop-gap measure."

"Oh," Kitty said. "It's a stop-gap measure."

"She's purrdy."

"Yeah, well you're freakin' her out gawkin' like that. She's gonna think you're a couple of psycho killers." I unclipped a bag of Ranch Doritos from the wall and tried to hand them to her. "Eat," I said. "Tam eat."

She shook her head proudly. "*Tam work! Tam help Chief!*" Flip-flop, flip-flop. I watched the rubber slap the bottoms of her russet heels as she went, flashing a glimpse of creamy instep and the comma curl of little toe.

"She wants Chief to keep her," Kitty explained, "so she works her ass off and starves."

"We'll take 'er," Wayne said. "I mean if yew don't want 'er."

I tried to get back to Eden. Seems a river ran through it. Then the mail came.

Mr. Duval M. Vogelpoll:
Immigration and Naturalization Service (INS) agents have recently discovered spurious claims of familial relationship to Vietnam veterans made on the part of some Vietnamese nationals. While genetic testing to determine relationship will soon be INS policy, such was not the case when you elected to sponsor Nguyen Minh Tam. Information leads the INS to suspect that you are the victim of fraudulent assertions. An INS agent will be calling on you soon to make an appointment for definitive DNA testing. This service is provided to you free by your government. The procedure is fast, simple, and performed in your home by a trained health care professional.
Sincerely,
Glen G. Glanders, Special Agent, Immigration and Naturalization Service

REVEREND PUGH POUNDED the pulpit and took in air with

great gasps that fell into cadence. Tam sat beside me, swallowed in the dress of a woman named Ruby, Ruby who drove away one booze and Barbital morning with the bar receipts from the night before. Ruby who left a still-fluid bottle of nail polish called Porno Red. Tam crossed her legs and dangled the fluorescent flip-flop from the glimmering tips of her toes. I tried to receive the preacher's words but could still see the dance of the pink and porno red out of the corner of my eye.

Ruby had also abandoned a pair of shoes when she fled, and I told Tam to wear them to church, and she had made a great show all that morning scooting around in the oversized pumps like a cross-country skier. She had been waiting for me in the truck when it was time to leave for church and kept her feet behind the transmission hump until we were nearly there.

"I told you to wear the shoes," I had said as we entered the parking lot.

"Cow shoes. Tam cow-woman?"

"It's winter and..." She shook her head obstinately, not wanting those words.

"*Tam cow-woman?*"

"No, Tam is not a cow-woman."

She held up her palms as though it were so simple. "Den no wear cow shoes." She looked out the window and said nothing for awhile. Then, when I'd turned off the ignition, "Chief ruv cow-woman?"

Brother Pugh bore down on me from the pulpit. I put my hand on Tam's knee to still her foot and tried to put it out of my mind. Tried to think about what Pugh was saying. Sister Heflin suddenly shouted that she'd recently shamed the depths of hell. "Eloi, Eloi. Lama sabbach thani," Brother Cox shouted. Tam scooted closer. She had a smell my nose turned to involuntarily, like a sleeping dog to frying bacon.

"I DON'T KNOW what you're trying to pull, Duval," the doctor said, "but it's not going to work."

"I'm not trying to pull anything. I just want you to check her out is all. You can do that, can't you? Cardiologists are qualified to give physicals, aren't they?"

Tam sat on the tissue paper of the examination table, her feet dangling. I touched her knee to make her be still.

"That's not the point. This girl doesn't have an appointment. You do."

"I pay cash."

"It doesn't work like that. What you're asking me would …" and he let the sentence go.

"Would what? Why're you so scared? What're you afraid of, chickenshit?"

"I can't believe we're communicating on this level."

"Then just check her out." I took the doctor's silence as acquiescence. "But there's another thing."

"What?"

"I want you to look into our blood and tell me if we're kin."

THE SEASONS CHURNED. Late winter brought the Collins twins to plow the garden patch, then sit at the bar and eat tenderloin sandwiches and watch Tam. It was easy to understand their fascination. Everything she did was like nothing anyone else did. The way she walked, the way she ate with sticks, the way she pushed the thick glasses up her little bump of a nose.

10 Snow blew in on the first day of spring but was gone the next day. Then the weather turned warm and Tam found some old seeds and decided to plant the spot the twins had tilled. The seeds were moldy and there would be many killing frosts before May, but it gave her something to do and she was so proud of her efforts I didn't have the heart to tell her she was wasting her time. Rose and Jack lay on the ground close by her, occasionally rising to follow as she moved down the row with her hoe, Johnny Walker choosing to stay on his feet and at her heels. You would think everything was fine to watch them. As though there was not a care in the world.

But Good Friday found me awake before dawn. For the second month I would have to take money from the bank to keep the Center open. Special Agent Glanders and Dr. Logan had called within an hour of each other the day before and their information, far from clearing anything up, complicated my confusion. I went to the bathroom and stood under the shower, thinking. Didn't come up with much. Then I stepped into the hall with a towel around my waist and everything that was in my mind was instantly expelled. Tam was there, and she was naked.

On both our parts there was the initial jaw-dropping shock of the unexpected. Then she gasped. She recoiled as if she had just come upon some loathsome thing. She turned her eyes like one unwillingly made privy to a shameful secret.

"It's okay," I called, as she ran to her room. A man whose chest has been cut and spread is a horrible sight.

An hour later, she joined me at the picnic table out by the river with two mugs of coffee. So we were going to act like nothing happened. Fine with me. The turkeys didn't respond to my rusty yelping, so I called to them as if I were a barred owl. "Whocooksforyou? whocooksforyouaallll?" A tom thundered back from up on the ridge and under the dim dome of the sky, Nguyen Minh Tam, wrapped in a blue blanket against the morning chill, was surprised by her own delight.

Her laughter was unforced and authentic and I realized I had never heard it before and from the looks of her, she herself had not heard it for awhile. The sound of it went into me. It infused me with something I hadn't felt in such a long time that I had almost forgotten what it was like. If I can make this girl laugh, I said to myself, and left the thought incomplete for a moment. If I can make this girl laugh then there is no telling what else I might be able to do. For the first time in a long time I felt hope, and though I knew the feeling would pass, I took the feeling in hand and turned it over and over to appreciate it for what it was while it was there. It was in this frame of mind that I dropped a cigarette next to her feet.

"Wight on that quean spot!" she said, mimicking what she'd heard me say.

I searched for the cigarette with my lighter and that is when it happened. It was then I went over the edge.

Her tiny toes were perfectly aligned atop her flip-flops, little to big, big to little, her nails sparkling like porno red jewels. It was like a vision. Like an epiphany. So beautiful, but more. It was like I had just found some long-lost, hard-sought artifact, some precious ruby tiara that had perhaps graced the brow of Cleopatra or Helen of Troy or the Virgin Mary and that somehow, someway, through an amazing series of unbelievable events, had found its way to the muddy banks of the Red River. I started talking as if she were about to go and words might have the power to hold her. I told her about whitetail bucks I'd hunted, about those I'd killed with guns and those I'd killed with arrows and those so clever no one ever killed them. I told her about catching bass, those with large mouths and those with small.

11

I told her about going after cottontail rabbits and fox squirrels and bobwhite quail and mourning doves with uncles and cousins who had been gone many years, though I told it like it happened only last fall. I told about hunting coons and possums with blue tick hounds and springer spaniels, about sitting around fires, drinking bonded whiskey with old men who believed ghosts were in the woods, but went there anyway. I told her about running a trotline, about muskrats, and mink, and fox and all the other animals that make it their job not to be seen by humankind.

She touched my chest. "Chief hurt?"

So we weren't going to ignore it after all.

"That's what our buddy the Doctor did for me. Wants to do it again. It was awful, Tam. Going to sleep, not knowing if you'll wake up. Then just laying there alone for days, unable to move. It's my heart. It's all this shit I've done all these years. It's come back to me, Tam. It's all come back. It was awful. Just laying there."

She put her hand on mine, and night passed into day.

"THIS FITS THE modus operandi to a T." Special Agent Glanders said. "This is exactly how the scam works." He dropped the creased photo of me and Lan on the bar. "In the wake of the war, Americans left millions of photographs in Vietnam. Millions of letters detailing the most personal information. The illegal alien gains access to this material somehow, hits the open sea, then, if they're lucky enough to get picked up, start parroting names and dates. In your case, Mr. Vogelpoll, we suspect you were also researched on the Internet. I believe you have a site detailing some kind of genealogy? When it is known you're not related, she'll start talking love. Or has that already happened? Look, your government only wants to protect you."

"I appreciate that, but like I said, she's not here now."

There was noise in the kitchen.

"What's that?"

"Probably a pitbull."

"Right. I'll just take a look."

"Wish you wouldn't."

He entered the kitchen and for a moment there was nothing. Then the ratta-tat-tat of sixty toenails. Glanders came through the door backpedaling. Jack Daniels and Irish Rose were snapping and snarling, but

Johnny Walker had the agent's leg and was thrashing like a shark.

"Dumbass!" one of the twins said. "He toldja not to go. An' weres yer warrant?"

"Yew'd best run," said the other. "I cain't hold these dogs no longer. I ain't able!"

I found Tam under my desk, all snot and tears. "Tam sawee! Tam sawee! Tam quean!" as her trickle spread over the floor.

I STAYED UP late that night.

I hate leaving things at loose ends, but sometimes you just can't figure it out. Sometimes you just don't know which way to turn or what to believe. In the hall, I stepped on something I thought was a sock until I turned on my light. White and glossy, Tam must have dropped them on her way from the shower. I picked them up. Not much there. Silky synthetic and a reinforced cotton panel. Soft. A fringe of lace. Soft. I held them to my face.

They'd been worn.

I took the scent and held it in. It was like a song forgot. It was that push-pull attraction of inevitable fate that used to make me throttle back on curves and walk ungunned through the jungle at night.

Her door was ajar.

Air slid by. Wisteria prematurely bloomed at her open window. Johnny, Jack and Rose glanced up when I pushed the door open. Tam lay on her back, partially wrapped in her blue blanket, brown legs crossed at the ankles. I recalled her naked. I reconstructed it. Rebuilt it in my mind. Her chest almost boyish. Her pubic patch no more than the width of a crow's feather and just as black. I cannot recall my exact choreography, but I came to kneel, my lips so close to Tam's pink soles that I shared their tender breath. I tried to remember what the Bible said about sins of lust, about David and Bathsheba and Samson and Delilah.

She was awake.

In her eyes I saw my twinned reflection kneeling in shameful silhouette before the light of the door, a huge, stuttering supplicant, vainly trying to explain how he'd had come to be prostate, panties in hand. I ran to my room and locked the door. I went straight to the Bible and read how God put the Tree of Good and Evil in the middle of Eden and filled it with the most beautiful fruit, and made it a rule that it was not to be eaten. And I

13

could not help but think how the whole thing was such a set-up.

THE NEXT MORNING I summoned Tam front and center.

Flip-flop, flip-flop. She looked at the floor like she'd done something wrong. I followed her glance down, then made myself turn away.

"I've made a list," I said, "and I want to go over it with you. 'One. Kitty will take Tam to buy clothes for Easter Sunday. Two. Two pairs of shoes will be purchased. A pair of oxfords for formal wear and a pair of high-top gym shoes for day to day. Three. Tam will wear shoes at all times. Four. Tam will keep clothes in drawers or in a separate clothes hamper that will also be purchased today.' Do you understand all of this, young lady?"

She nodded, totally baffled.

When Kitty came I sent them on their way with the last of my cash.

WE LEFT EARLY the next morning for the Easter Sunrise service, Kitty having dressed Tam like a Catholic school girl in a white blouse, hunter green sweater, and black watch pleated skirt.

"Where's your glasses?" I said when we were almost there.

She held up her palms and shrugged.

"Don't give me that. Where are they? I bought those glasses for you to wear. Are they in your purse?"

She unsnapped her empty new purse and pretended to search.

"Where are they then? Leave 'em at home again?"

She nodded gravely. "Yes. Reave at home again."

"That's not where they belong, is it?"

"No," she said, shaking her head. "Bewrong on Tam's nose."

"That's right. We've talked about this before, haven't we?"

The church was crowded and we stood in the back looking for an empty spot. "Up front," I said, "next to the preacher's wife." On a table behind the altar were pitchers, plastic wash pans, and rolls of paper towels.

Errant strands of hair brushed my face when I leaned to her ear. "I think we might have communion," I said. "He'll say we're drinking blood but it ain't. Just do what everyone else does."

But it wasn't communion.

"Now the head of each family," Reverend Pugh informed the congregation, "will do as Christ did when He washed the feet of His disciples before his martyrdom."

I shot a glance at Tam, who was clueless but became interested when Pugh himself came down from the pulpit to lead off the ritual. With a snapping and cracking of joints, he knelt before his portly spouse, removed her sensible shoes, positioned the basin, and poured a few ceremonial drops atop her corpulent appendage. He handed the pitcher back to the usher, then dried the dampness with a paper towel, performing the entire rite without once touching his skin to hers.

He pushed the basin toward me and I made some utterance, some stumbling attempt at an excuse the ushers didn't want to hear. So I knelt and Tam, as Mrs. Pugh had done before her, offered her foot. I pulled the stiff string of her new saddle oxfords. The shoe said "hush" when I slipped it off. I peeled the white sock down under her heel, over the narrow brown bridge, then off those tropical little digits upon which childish fragments of polish still adhered, shining in the stained-glass light. Free from restraint, there was a bit of movement, an involuntary wiggle. An usher behind me sighed. I took her gently in my hands. She was moist and sticky like candy apple and smelled of new leather.

I really don't know what happened next. For a moment I thought I was having a heart attack. Peripheral vision constricted. Sounds drowned in a white drone that seemed to spring from my inner ear. The universe condensed into the barely perceptible throb of her pulse radiating from her sole into my fingers, joining me to the very chambers of her living heart, dark and wet and warm, containing secrets that predate language and so can't be told even if known. I looked into her eyes, completing the circuit. Then did that which I desired.

WHEN MORAVIAN MISSIONARY John Vogelpohl found the Black Jacksons in 1732, they had a ceremonial tradition of circular dancing. No one knows what the dance was like other than that it lasted hours and resulted in frenzy. Alafair Jackson has taken the idea and made it his own.

Jim Morrison is singing *L.A. Woman* on the jukebox and Alafair has a circle out on the floor. He has his arm around Tam's shoulder and she has her arm around him and he's teaching her the steps of the dance, which have always eluded me. The toes touch. The heels touch. The balls of the feet touch. Then the music breaks wildly and she's dancing like she's been doing it forever. She's wearing the jeans I bought her, and the red boots too. Her tapered shirt features two identical embroidered cowboys facing off on each other, one over each breast, identical lassos circling aloft. Her eyes are now blue, thanks to contacts, and she goes around and around and every time she looks at me. She has become more than beautiful. She has something that sends light out and draws light in. L.A. is just a town out west.

Kitty collects dollars and pours bourbon. The weather has held and the Iron Horsemen have fired up their oil-streaked twin-Vs and are now drunk and disorderly. A good looking kid named Seth with a girl hanging from his arm comes up, his hand scabby with a new tattoo.

"I thought I told you to never get a tat a judge can see."

"Why should I listen to you?" he says, but he lets me keep my hand on his awhile.

"How's your mom?"

"Good. She asks about you. She heard you were going for surgery."

"Tell her I'm fine. Tell her I asked about her."

An Iris DeMent song comes on, sad and slow, and Seth takes his girl by the waist and pulls her onto the floor, and I am alone. A man asks Tam to dance and she looks to see that I'm watching, shakes her head resolutely, then sits down with a glass of orange juice and a couple of women who suspect the reason she is so imbued with light. I take the opportunity to slip away.

Outside it is warm and dark and raining. It is so dark. I can make my way to the river only because I know where it is and I stop when I hear its rushing.

But there is light after all and my eyes slowly adjust. Downstream broken pylons of an old train trestle stand like some riverine Stonehenge, and I watch the water flow, charting its course, thinking how it comes and how it goes. To the Red, the Kentucky, the Ohio, and on down the Mississippi to the Gulf of Mexico. Evaporation. On Africa, rain. Then back again as a hurricane. On the hills, a trace of color where leaves are coming on, the rose of redbud, the white of dogwood, a splotch of cedar, the skeletal hands of sycamores. It is dark. So dark. And there is no one but me to witness sprouts break the earth and rain join the river on its way to the sea.

The Fall

JACKSON CLEFT IS a mere scratch on the topographical map, lost amid the swirling contour lines of the Red River Gorge. In width, less than the span of a football field at its widest point. In length, 385 yards from fountainhead to pinchpoint, where facing cliffs crowd in on one another, squeezing some velocity into the small stream before it spews into the pool of a natural stone basin. Reed McCampbell stares at his reflection in that pool, wondering what kind of monster he has become.

The pool is dark and McCampbell doesn't know how deep it is. After heavy rains, runoff from the cliffs turns the stream into a torrent, and locals claim you can hear boulders banging on the bottom of the basin like musket fire. But this is from the same people who hear the Greenman crying at night and see the light moving on the mountain. McCampbell has been in this slit in the earth during storms and, while the water rose violently, the only sound he heard was of its rushing.

To be sure, that unapproachable question that has lurked so long in the dark wings of his mind has recently stormed to center stage, screaming its awful answer. There is no denying it. At the end of the day—after all his self-justification and claims of mitigating circumstances—he is what he is. *Mr. McCampbell,* Reed imagines a prosecuting attorney saying, *on May 1, at 4:30 in the afternoon, at the Moontown furnace ruin, did you...* And the lawyer would fill in the lewd details, using the proper words, the dictionary words, but repeating them, driving them home so that the jurors would have a clear image of what happened. Without doubt there would be a gasps from the jury box. Heavy-set matrons would turn to look at him and wish they had never heard of Reed McCampbell and his unspeakable perversions.

But your honor, Reed could say, *the girl is still a virgin.* And all that would do is underscore the unnaturalness of his acts.

McCampbell chooses his steps carefully on the mossy stones as he passes around the pool and into the Cleft. It is a world the sun sees sparingly, a moist fern world of sheer rock and labyrinthine folds of red sandstone. He looks to a high rock shelter, officially field site CMNH-15UNI (dubious), where, he told friends, he means to photograph petroglyphs.

McCampbell slides his backpack off and changes into climbing shoes. He has climbed the cliff dozens of times, always with the help of a top-roped belay, and has always thought the 5.10 rating was overblown, though the route has its moments, particularly under the shelter where an overhang jutts out like an anvil head. The first few handholds, though—covered with chalk so many climbers have held them—are old friends that seem to lift him onto the rock as if gravity has been suspended. He climbs ten or twelve vertical feet and rests, arms locked straight, pushing his weight into the rock. A five-foot slab of nearly featureless stone stretches before him. He looks down. Falling from such a height probably wouldn't even break a bone. He gathers a breath and goes, tensing his fingers against any purchase, smearing his toes onto any irregularity. No sweat. He gets over it fast.

He looks down at his pack on the ground. He should have brought his camera. How can a person take photos without a camera? Too late now. He steps onto a five-inch ledge and begins transverse walking to a large vertical crack—a chimney formation—where he can wedge himself isometrically. He keeps his cheek against the rock as he inches along, concentrating on niches, searching them out with his fingers, remembering them from climbs past. His hand closes on a symmetrical protuberance, a bud not big enough to fill his palm. He wonders if he should have written a letter.

APRIL JACKSON WASN'T a giggler. And the slight smile that curled on her lips as she listened to her classmate bespoke amusement more than kindness.

"Mr. McCampbell," Tiffany said. "I gotta see Miz Peters cause I'm planin' to *commit suicide*." Tiffany wore the food stamp carapace of a woman three times her age.

April rolled her eyes, picked up a letter from Reed's desk and pulled a crease down the middle with her thumb and forefinger. "How ya gonna do it?" she asked. A boy named Zack leaned in April's direction and she threw an elbow into his ribs, causing him to shake his pimple-studded head like he was waking in a strange place.

"Do what?" Tiffany said.

"Kill yourself." April concentrated on folding the paper. "You said you had a plan."

Her blue-jeans hung low and her t-shirt stopped short, exposing a sliver of brown belly, the southern rim of her navel and, even farther south, a glimpse of lace cross-stitching on the waistband of her underpants. She'd started out a little slovenly this morning, a sleepy girl dragged from bed at an ungodly hour to bear the indignities of a school bus, but her Cocoa Puffs were working now so she was firing on all cylinders.

"I ain't got that far yet."

April glanced at Reed, then back to the paper she was folding. "Aren't there guns at your house? We got guns stuck all over. We got so many guns I go to look for the clicker and find a fucking gun."

"April," Reed said.

"Sorry, Mr. McCampbell. I just can't believe Tiff can't get her hands on a gun."

Tiffany's brow knotted slightly. "Well…" she said. "Bubby has a shotgun."

"There ya go. Bubby's shotgun."

"That's enough, April."

"I'm just trying to help, Mr. McCampbell." Her dimples were in full play. "Stick the barrel in your mouth and push the trigger with your big toe."

"*April.*"

"Anyways," Tiffany said. "Can I *please* go see Miz Peters, Mr. McCampbell? *Pleease?* Ain't there a law that says you hafta let me go if I say I'm gonna kill myself?"

"That's in West Virginia," April said, running her fingers over another crease in the paper. "In Kentucky they let you blow your goddamn head off!"

"*April!*"

"Please, Mr. McCampbell. *Pleeease.*"

"Tiffany," April said, "you know good and well Mr. McCampbell never changes his mind after he says no. He's told us that a million times. That's how he discourages whining. But it ain't working with ole Tiff, is it Mr. McCampbell?" Under April's spell again, Zack actually touched her shoulder with his. She threw up her elbow once more and the boy came to again, mystified as to the nature of his infraction but resigned to accept any punishment that came his way.

The bell rang.

"Get to your seats," Reed said. "Beat it. All of you."

April alone stood her ground as the "Star-Spangled Banner" played, then ignored the Pledge, continuing to fold the paper.

Hand over his heart, Reed looked at her, at her hair, thick and long and dark with streaks of brown and even auburn, her eyes slightly Asian— though not enough to tell unless you knew—her mouth not Negroid but neither having truck with the thin-lipped variety worn by her Scotch-Irish peers. It took the whole world to make April May Jackson, every race, creed and continent, "with liberty and justice for all."

She held the paper quadruped before her. "What is it?" she demanded.

Perhaps it was her simplicity that first sparked the fire. She wore no makeup. None needed. No perfume. She smelled just fine. She was a creature only distantly related to the adult women Reed knew, women who could not possibly be so elegantly simple. Reed recalled undressing Sharon Peters, coming up against an array of pantyhose, slips and pads. April, he imagined, could be naked in seconds. T-shirt over the head, kick off the clogs, single shove down from the hips, and there she is, child Venus, bringing a tiny foot out of white cotton panties.

"It's a memo from Dr. Macintosh I haven't read," Reed said.

"What kind of *animal*?"

"Dog," he said. "It's a dog."

She looked gravely from side to side, then spoke low, conspiratorially. "I'm so sorry, but I'm afraid you're wrong. You see, it's a horse. A horse named Dobbin."

That was early on, and months would pass before he went over the edge.

IT ISN'T A NATURAL thing to do—to put your hand in some dark crack in the earth and probe the recess for something to hold onto— and many gym climbers have no stomach for it. There are spiders galore, a rare bat, and spurious stories of snake dens, but McCampbell feels a kind of relief as he wedges his shoulder and leg into the crevice. He's in the elevator now. He can get some altitude.

He inches up the crack, bridging between knees and back, flaring the angle of his thighs as the width of the chimney gradually widens until it is greater than the distance between his feet and hips. He continues bridging, hands opposing feet, pressing out against the rock, until the stone again closes in on his back and he is once more wedged in the security of the two slabs. He lay his head back against the cold stone and exhales as if to rid his body of all its content.

Does he want her because she is so young or in spite of the fact? Legally, a moot point. A distinction without a difference. He moves on up the ever-narrowing chimney.

Months before he even touched her, he couldn't help thinking about her, in fact could think of nothing else—what he might say, for instance, if she said this, or what he might do if she did that, and that was what led him to seek help—his sheer inability to think of anything else. So concerned that no word of his problem get out, McCampbell drove to Lexington for treatment and didn't bother to see if his insurance would cover it. The agency was in a bad neighborhood in a rundown building, the waiting room of which was full of unwashed people who sat on metal folding chairs and seemed to be either sad or angry. On the peeling wall was a poster of a kitten clinging to a clothesline. "Hang in there, baby!" the poster read. Twenty minutes after his appointment was to begin, a weeping girl with a biracial baby emerged from the hallway followed by a woman who carried a clipboard.

"Dan O'Connor? Is Dan here?"

"Here," McCampbell said.

The room they went to was the size of a prison cell, containing two chairs separated by a coffee table with a box of Puffs on it. In one corner, file cabinets. Against the wall, a desk with sundry stacks of paper, a well-worn copy of the *Diagnostic Standards*, and several audiocassette tapes. Over the desk hung a feathered dream catcher and a poster of a handsomely weathered Chief Seattle. *The earth does not belong to us, but we to it.*

"Is this being taped?" McCampbell asked.

"Don't worry about that," the woman said, gesturing for him to take a seat.

A liar's answer, he thought. *Notice, ladies and gentlemen of the jury, the defendant was not told that he was not being taped, only that he shouldn't worry about it.*

"So the answer is no?"

Some jewelry the woman wore jingled as she smoothed the pleats of her ankle-length red skirt. "No," she smiled. "We don't tape sessions." A crystal dangled from a necklace into the scoop of her peasant blouse. "This is confidential. Nothing will go beyond these four walls. So the whole truth can be told. Must be told. No lies. Not even the lies we tell ourselves. My name is Kieva," she said offering her jangling hand.

"Dan O'Connor," McCampbell said.

"So why don't you tell me why we're here, Dan?"

He wondered where April was, what she was doing, what she was wearing. "I've become obsessed with something," he said. "I think about it every waking moment."

"It?"

"Her." He wondered who she was with, what words her tongue was forming.

"And when you sleep?"

"I dream of her."

"And the nature of those dreams? Sexual?"

This is a mistake, he told himself. "Some of them are."

"What percentage of your dreams would you say are sexual?"

"Ninety," he said. "I'd say ninety percent are sexual."

Kieva made a note. "What percentage of your dreams are violent?"

"What? None of them. Why would you ask that?"

Kieva looked up. "So your impulses don't entail any aspect of abuse?"

He didn't answer.

"Is she a celebrity or someone you know personally?"

"I know her."

"Who is she?"

McCampbell shook his head.

"Perhaps a friend's wife? Maybe a relative? To be sure, someone forbidden. Someone taboo. Someone to whom you can't make your feelings known."

McCampbell felt his face blanch. Kieva sat back in her chair. "If you're not ready, that's okay, but you do need to tell. Let's go at it another way. Was there one particular instance that triggered the obsession? One central event that you think back to as the beginning? Without divulging her identity, could you tell me about that instance?"

McCampbell replayed the moment in his mind as he had ten thousand times before.

"There was no such instance," he said.

"If you want me to help you, Dan, you have to level with me."

"My name's not Dan, and I can't bring her here. Not even in conversation."

McCampbell stood, took the cash for the full fifty minutes from his wallet, and dropped it on the table. "I'm sorry," he said.

It was raining but trying to snow. He sat in his truck letting the engine warm, listening to a song about good lovin' gone bad on the radio.

There was a tapping on the window. Kieva. McCampbell cracked the window. "I'm sorry for wasting your time, okay? It just wasn't a good idea."

"Please listen," she said, slipping an envelope through the window. "If you weren't comfortable you're right to leave, but please seek counseling elsewhere. Do it for her. *For her*. Because sometimes I feel things. And I feel horrible things now. Awful things…"

McCampbell shoved the Ford into gear. "Step back please." At the first stoplight he opened the envelope and found his money and the business cards of three psychologists and someone identified as a practitioner/priest.

FIFTY-FIVE FEET ABOVE the base of the cliff, the chimney squeezes in. If Reed is to climb higher, he must execute a lieback, hook his fingers onto the edge of the crack while his feet, wedged in below, apply opposing force. With such balancing of tension, he can inch his way up to the overhang that guards access to CMNH-15UN1 (dubious).

It may have started with her gym bag.

"Can I keep this behind your desk?" she asked the first week of school. The bag said "Adidas" on the side and had a pair of Nikes tied to the straps with blaze orange shoestrings. "I run cross-country and I'm in your homeroom and I'm here last period, too, so I'll pick it up then."

He said OK, and she tossed the bag in the corner, and that was that.

The pheromonal Trojan Horse was through the gate. Cross country gave way to basketball, and basketball to track, and the gym bag mostly lay behind McCampbell's desk, imparting through aerial osmosis the alluring ambrosia of April's body.

This was the theory he had come to think of as "Reductionist April," giving her the animalistic power of a freshly-fecund female but nothing more, breaking the whole thing down into rut behavior in which he was the hapless old buck pursuing a hot little doe on the precipice of first heat. It was not a theory he particularly believed in, but it was a theory.

The triggering event Kieva guessed at occurred on one of those unusually warm late winter days that cause the young and the foolish to hope that spring is here to stay. April had long since quietly taken to sitting at his desk while he was standing before the class. After she left he would find his drawers had been rearranged, or a message was on his computer, or she would leave drawings on Post-it notes stuck in unusual places he might not find for weeks. But on March fifteenth, April discovered that the paper hole punch cut out tiny heart-shaped pieces of confetti.

"See-ya-later-alligator," she said, walking out after everyone else had left. The floor around his desk was littered with dozens of tiny yellow hearts.

"Whoa! What's this?"

She stepped back and put her books on his desk, and it struck him that this was one of her artifices, something she had planned. "Look," she said, slipping several Post-it sheets into the punch, "I can make a bunch at a time."

The hearts fluttered like snowflakes, brushing down the front of her t-shirt and jeans, and as the hearts fell, she made a movement, a slight arching of her back, perhaps to draw attention to her breasts, but having the effect of pulling up the hem of her shirt, exposing her navel, wherein, as if on cue, a single yellow heart came to nestle. He stared, transfixed, for he didn't know how long.

"Mr. McCampbell?" she said. "People are walking by the door. They're seeing this."

"Oh," he said, stupidly. "It's just so…so…*beautiful*."

"Thank you," she said as though the compliment was overdue. "Can I go now? I promise to bring it when I come back."

"Sure."

"Sure?"

"Sure."

It was a week later he met with Kieva.

THE ART OF CLIMBING is finding that point between one's comfort level and one's point of unacceptable fear and playing in the gray area, ever pushing back the darker shades. Usually, this is done with a rope.

Reed McCampbell swings out onto the face of the rock like a barn door. There's an updraft, a rarefied breeze from below bearing the fragrance of earth. Right hand slides up, left hand slides up, left foot slides up, right foot slides up. Inch by inch by terrible inch, he can feel the tendons in his joints stretch, the muscles warm. He looks down. The sun is setting and the base of the cliff is muted in shadow. He spits, and counts the seconds—onemississippi, twomississippi, three...—until the white speck disappears.

The phase he had come to think of as "The Adoration" began a couple of weeks before school was out. He would put his class on worksheets or clank in a videocassette and sit next to April at this desk and look at her, at her perfect skin, at the fine hair that curled at the nape of her neck when she wore her hair up, at her glistening pink tongue when she talked. He studied her facial expressions, her quirky mannerisms, the way she picked out the orange Skittles to eat first. He would find excuses to hand her pencils or paper clips, and their fingers would touch, lingering a second longer than they should. Students noticed. Teachers noticed. So what? He was enthralled.

Think of it always, speak of it never. Isn't that what the French say? And they know about these things. Any good lawyer would tell you to shut up. Just shut up. But he couldn't, and one day, as she lingered after the others had gone to their buses, he spoke.

"April," he said with such a tone of fatalistic finality that she looked at him as if she expected him to tell her that he loved her. For a moment he considered saying exactly that, not because it was right, but because it was the truth. "What's happening here?"

He knew as soon as he asked that she should plead ignorance, act dumb, say, What do you mean?

"You like to look at me," she said. "Why? Why do you look at me that way?"

He wasn't quite dumbstruck because he had thought of the answer before. Still, he took time to gather his thoughts, then paused a moment before putting them out. "I see beautiful women—girls—all the time in magazines and on TV," he said, "but I've never known, really known, someone as beautiful, as devastatingly beautiful, as you. And what I know about you is that your aloofness, your standoffishness, isn't arrogance or trying to be demure. It's an old-fashioned virtue. It's class. You act as if you're better than other people, and the plain truth is, you are."

He wondered how much she understood.

"I like when you look at me," she said. "It makes me feel special. Like I have power."

"You'd better go."

"No," she said, stepping toward him. "Not yet."

Her tongue was soft and wet and tasted of orange Skittles.

ON A PORTRUDING LEDGE just below the overhang, climbers have carved initials and dates. Some day the rock will join its brothers on the ground, maybe in a million years, maybe in a second, and then it will be no boast to have one's initials there. As anchor scars attest, the ledge is a good place to rest before taking on the overhang, or before deciding a discrete rappel is the better part of valor. Reed pulls himself onto the ledge and doesn't look down. Climbers should never look down, Reed tells the kids in Climb Club. There's no reason to. Everything that concerns a climber is within reach.

The night of the day he kissed her he couldn't sleep. He knew he would be hauled into the office first thing the next day and fired. Perhaps the sheriff would be there and he would be arrested too. Maybe April herself, crying, having considered how he had used her and feeling dirty and violated.

But the sheriff wasn't parked in the parking lot. And no one was waiting for him at the door. No one was waiting in his room. He sat on his desk and watched the kids from the Massieville bus file in. April was not with them. Maybe she was in the office, he thought. Maybe with the guidance counsellors. Maybe her brother was there too, barely being restrained from tearing down the hall in the direction of Reed's room.

"Can I get a drink?" Bobby Shortandpudgy asked, having just walked past the water fountain outside the door.

"Drink?" Reed said absently. Every other day he told the boy to sit down.

Bobby shifted his soft weight, the departure from the script making him nervous. "I guess I can wait," he said uneasily.

High heels echoed in the hall—*click! click!! click!!!*—growing closer and closer.

"I gotta use the phone," Tiffany said.

April suddenly appeared in the doorway tottering on stiletto sandals. She paused, regained her balance, then sauntered into the room. Her black skirt stopped at mid-thigh and the morning air had had its way with her nipples under her sleeveless gray sweater. There was no way her mother would let her out of the house like that. That was why she was tardy. She'd had been in the restroom changing.

"Hardwick's abusing me," Tiffany said, "and I gotta report him before he victimizes another."

"*Hard*dick?" April said, swaying like a newborn colt. "What the hell kind of name is *Hard*dick?" Her eyeliner curled up at the ends, giving her eyes the effect of wearing little horns.

"He's my mom's boyfriend and his name is Hard*wick*." Tiffany turned back to Reed. "They gotta tip line. You just leave it on the machine. I'm gonna say he uses drugs too."

The intercom sizzled in prelude to the "Star Spangled Banner."

"Beat it," Reed said. "All of you."

April steadied herself against the desk and held a foot up for inspection. "Like 'em? The *shoes*. They're Rachael's. I pierced her eyebrow last night."

The anthem played and April sat at Reed's desk, kicked off Rachael's shoes, unlocked his drawer and began putting coins in rolls. The money was from a candy sale fundraiser the Climb Club had just wrapped up. Reed had already converted the funds to bills out of his own pocket and made the deposit in the club's account, leaving this bag of pennies and nickels that April put into rolls during the odds and ends of time she was in his room.

Reed needed to enter attendance into his computer, but when he tried she seemed to be in the way. She seemed to be everywhere he needed to go or even look, expanding in all directions like the universe, her hair, her legs, her arms, her painted fingers, her painted toes, the penumbra of

27

her perfume. All of it moving, writhing, creating breezes that brushed against his hands and face and entered his head through his mouth and nose and took his breath away and filled his brain with such alarm that he forgot why he was behind his desk in the first place.

"We'll use this money this summer," she whispered. "I'll say I'm going to Ashley's and we'll rent a canoe over in Morgan. We'll do it on a weekday and there won't be *nobody* on the river. We'll swim and build a fire and have a cookout with *beer*."

Reed made a sound that wasn't a word. April mimicked it perfectly. "Goofball," she said, slipping fifty pennies into the roll.

Dr. MacIntosh read coach-written announcements detailing the victories and defeats of various athletic teams, ending each account with a personal comment. "Way to go Mohawks!" or "Better luck next time fellas!"

"'*Fellas*'," April snorted. "Doughboy's such a dildoe." She thought the principal looked like the Pillsbury trademark. "If he's a doctor why ain't he at the hospital?"

April swiveled in the chair and reached for the tape dispenser, showing him as she did. She showed him and he looked. He could do nothing else.

"He's not a doctor of medicine, if that's what you mean. Listen, about yesterday—"

"What's he a doctor of? Dildoeology?"

"About yesterday…"

April put his glasses on the end of her nose, spun once in his chair and came around as someone else. "Yas, yas!" she stroked her chin. "*Yas*terday. Yas. I've been meaning to speak with you about *yass*terday. Yasssss…. Shit! Don't look now but Casper's here."

Macintosh stood in the door, his milky ears growing crimson. "What was that?"

"What was *what?*"

Red spread over Macintosh's face. "Let's go, young lady. To my office. Now! Mr. McCampbell, would you come in when you finish with homeroom?"

Dr. Robert Macintosh's office was paneled in knotty pine and bore the olfactory evidence of its occupant's losing battle with body odor. The curtains, the carpets, the Styrofoam soil of the plastic phloxes—even the wood-chip potpourri in the Longabarger basket—were all ingrained with

28

his Altoid fueled fetor. Vapors of his cologne merged with the vapors of his colon. Wisps of Odor Eaters mingled with the effluvium of his nylon sheathed feet. And it all had fused into the physical objects of the room, because the man smelled so bad, and had been there so long.

The relationship between the principal and April had obviously deteriorated in the few minutes it took Reed to join them. Macintosh was at his desk fuming, framed photos of his double-chinned family grinning in juxtaposition behind him. April, her long limbs brown and bare, graced the hot seat like a pagan princess, petulant and bored with the dreary histrionics of an odious missionary. Reed sat in a chair and tried not to glance at her thighs, her knees, her ankles, her feet. He tried to ignore her elegant fingers. Tried not to remember the electricity they could deliver. Tried to block out their drum, drum, drumming of tedious intent upon the turquoise plastic of the arm of her chair.

"Would you stop that," Macintosh said.

"What?"

"Drumming your fingers."

"Why? Does it bother you?"

"*Stop it!*"

She drummed once more, then slowly crossed her legs and let that sandal dangle, dangle, dangle from the tips of her toes.

"Mr. McCampbell," Macintosh said, "our Little Miss here doesn't get it. She has *no idea* what kind of trouble she's in!" He picked up her file folder. "Will you look at the number of write-ups our Little Miss has racked up! And this whole thing started out as a simple dress-code violation and has now snowballed into something *entirely* different!"

April sighed. "If you're going to send me to the ACE room I wish you'd just do it."

He was like a thermometer dropped in a boil. "Why you little.... Get out! Go to ACE right now!"

So the day went on without April. Reed was getting ready to leave at three when she barged into his room in a two-piece Spandex number.

"I meant to show you this earlier but Beluga Bob had to pee in the tea." She produced a photo album from her book bag. "It's got some really old pictures. Some of Dad when he was a kid. My mom put it together but I've been updating it." She handed him the album. "You can look at it, but I have to take it home today. I'm staying for open gym so I can pick it up at four. I mean if you have to work on grades or something and are gonna be around." She looked down at Reed's briefcase, ready to go.

Hand it back. Say you won't be around. Not now, not ever. Tell her you have to leave because it is the best thing for both of you. "Yeah," he said, taking the scrapbook. "I'll be here at four."

A few minutes later, on the basketball court in the parking lot below Reed's window, nine boys were getting up a game. Shirts and skins. The tenth player was April, chosen as a putative skin.

Swiveling back to his desk, the photo album fell open to a pressed rose, its once red petals presaging the dun to which the paper aspired, all dimensions flattened by time except for the thorns, which inflicted indentations on a half dozen pages in either direction. The flower marked a page bearing perhaps the last photo of April's family intact, Duval and Tam and April and her half-brother Buck, sitting at a table with piles of food in front of them. Mashed potatoes, fried chicken, green beans, corn on the cob, slaw. Buck is scowling. Tam is smiling. And Duval has April in his lap. The old man had beaten his prognosis by years but the brutality of the struggle tells on his face. Yet there is discernable pride in his eyes. I drank life to the lees, he seems to say, and for my final act, I leave this perfect child.

The page opposite has been newly added to the binder and features a single photograph, centered in a carefully hand-drawn frame. Here is Duval in healthier days, his massive arm around the shoulder of a skinny kid of nineteen. Beneath, in April's careful hand, "Duval Jackson and Reed McCampbell."

Reed looked out the window. April was bringing the ball down. Just over the mid-court line, a defender, a chubby boy who played tackle on the football team, picked her up and she turned her back, thrust her butt into his soft middle, faked right, drove left, then fired the ball to a teammate at the bottom of the lane, pushing the pass out from her chest with her right hand, the trajectory fast and flat. The boy put the ball up and it bounced around the hoop without going in. The rebound went to a shirtless boy with nascent chest hair.

"Chad!" April shouted from the outside, holding her hand aloft. He passed off to her and she shot. The ball bounced off the rim and the game sped to the other end of the court, leaving this suddenly smitten lad, this heart-pierced Chad, standing alone beneath the undefended basket, watching April run.

Reed turned a few pages. Tam had saved everything. Letters from the Immigration Service. Letters she had written Duval from the refugee camp.

Outside his window, April brought the ball down again, bouncing it through a puddle, passing off then breaking for the corner. The ball was worked to Chad, who drove for a lay-up but at the last moment bounce passed to April, who faked with her head, drew a jump from her sluggish defender, then broke to the basket for the bucket. It's high fives all around, even from guys on the other team. Everyone wanted to touch April's hand.

The album contained lists Duval had made. Drawings. Diagrams. School photos of April. School photos of Duval. Group pictures showing him taller than his classmates. Darker. Duval playing football. Duval playing baseball. Duval with a string of small mouth bass. Duval with dead buck and 30-06. Duval in Vietnam with M-16. Duval astride Electra-Glide. Jesus, he was a handsome man.

"And what I want to know is just how did you get up here, young lady?" The screech of Wilma McAdams broke Reed's thoughts.

"I'm here to see Mr. McCampbell," Reed heard April say.

"We can as*sume* who you are here to see. The question at hand is *how* did you get here?"

The magnets holding the interior doors automatically lost their charge at 3:15, shutting off the wings of the building. He leaned into the hall and April seized upon the power shift. "Don't *assume* anything. *Assume* only makes and an *ass* of *u* and *me*. Mostly you."

"Why…! I *never*…!"

"That's enough, April. It's okay, Mrs. McAdams. She's here to pick something up."

But Wilma McAdams was not finished sputtering. "But…how did she get here? Students aren't allowed on the fire stairs. How else could she have gotten here?"

Wilma's nose was her most striking feature. Large and sprouting manly hairs, it seemed to always be sampling the world's worst odors.

"I guess I must've taken the fire stairs then."

"I said, *That's enough April*," Reed said. She flipped her mane and strode through his door, sparing not the wiggle beneath the Spandex. Wilma stood alone, stranded on the dry rock of principle, disgustedly assessing April's shifting liquefaction, nostrils flaring as though assailed by the rankest

Limburger.

Inside the door, April mimicked him. *"'That's enough April!'* Did you catch the facial I shot her? I hate her goddamn guts, the old Snout. Bet she's still out there. *Listening!* Like we'd do anything here, right? Did you see that Davy Crockett picture? It's funny." She was doing this thing with her hair, leaning her head one way, then flipping back the other. Finally she sheaved it all together in an elastic scrunchy.

"You in the coonskin hat? Yeah, I saw that. Listen, about—"

"Sit down and I'll show you."

Okay. He sat at his desk and she stood beside him. She drank water from his cup and he could hear it go down. She sat the cup before him. On the rim he could see where her lips had been. She leaned over the album, smelling of sweat and apple blossom body splash, pushed her hair back over her neck, and turned the pages. "There it is."

April, a year old, wore a souvenir coonskin hat and a sagging diaper under a full tummy, holding on to a battered muzzle loader that easily predated the Civil War, a dripping smile showing a new tooth, the steadying denim clad legs of someone behind her. Waddles of fat on her thighs. Fat on the tops of her little feet, one of which is turned on its side.

"Look at my belly button. I had an outie then. And look at it here," she bent again, ensnaring tendrils of hair grazing his cheek, his neck, turning the pages to another photo, this one of a leaner child of maybe three sitting naked in a plastic wading pool. "You can see it starting to go in. Going, going, gone!" With the last word, she slapped her own bare midriff. And there it was. A perfect oval. A soft swirl then surprisingly deep, the lower curvature slightly rimmed and containing a tiny jewel of perspiration. A barely visible trace of golden fleece, delicate hairs growing together like so many vertical Vs, disappeared beneath the material that lay so lightly on her skin.

He kissed her again.

He kissed her there.

APRIL PULLED HIM from her belly by his ears. The act was harsh and painful and took Reed by surprise. "Buck's here," she said, and Reed became aware of the bass notes of a motorcycle in the parking lot. "Listen," she said, "can you meet me at the furnace in an hour? What time is it?" She picked up his wrist. "What the hell's this? Sixteen ten.

Great. Well General McCampbell, report to the Moontown furnace at seventeen ten. Okay? *Okay? You gonna be there?"* He made some indication he would and she saluted and was gone.

He went to the window and waited to watch her walk into the parking lot. Buck revved the old Flathead, then killed it, which seemed to signal kids to gather around. Shirtless and hard, his black hair was almost as long as April's. Then April appeared and straddled the bike behind her brother, who raised his hips high and came down on the kick start with the heel of his broken down boot. April took the cigarette from his mouth and put it in her own and everyone watched them roar away in a cloud of burnt oil.

Reed turned away bewildered, hardly believing what had just happened. Hardly able to think at all. He looked at his watch. He guessed he had time for a fast shower.

THE OVERHANG LOOMS above him, guarding the mouth of the rock shelter. Floor midden proved millennia of human habitation. From Paleo-Indians to the Civil War, people who thought they had something to protect had sought security above the jutting rocks, had defended what they had with clubs and spears and guns against those covetous enough, or desperate enough, that they would set their lives on any chance, to mend or end, even unto a frontal assault of such a formidable stronghold.

Over the centuries the scene must have played out with weary regularity. Women and children in the recesses of the shelter, supporting the men any way they could—passing up rocks, sharpening sticks, pouring powder into muzzleloaders—and sometimes the invaders still won. That was in the midden too. A change of hands. A change of culture. And the defeated defenders? And their babies and their women? The rocks so far below showed no evidence, but then there are the animals to bear that proof away.

Reed McCampbell takes hold on the cresting sandstone wave, wedging his feet into what was left of the chimney crack. He leans back off his muscles, letting his skeleton take the weight.

Showered and shaved, Reed had parked in the ditch off Moontown Road and walked down the hollow on a raised levee that'd once carried railroad tracks to the furnace. Any trace of the village of Moontown was usually covered by the oak and maple of the National Forest, but on that early spring day, when last fall's leaves had been beaten limp and the foliage of spring had yet to come on in full, the ghost of Moontown emerged. There was the hint of foundation stones and streets. The mouth of an open well. In the leafmold, bricks and chunks of coal. There was the remnant of a rock wall and a patch of periwinkle or English ivy gone spindly and small. Farther from the levee, the garden plans of the long dead sprang forth in brief resurrection as lilacs and hyacinths traced the outlines of sidewalks and homes now gone.

April would come riding her bike up from Massieville. She was late, and for a moment he found himself hoping she wouldn't come. Then he heard a motor screeching like a chain saw. She was on a dirt bike, hair flying like a flag, wearing the same blue Spandex she had played basketball in. She steered straight for him, laughing, then swerving at the last moment, going airborne off the levee and into a clumsy landing below.

"I woulda been here sooner but that butthole Dwayne called off and Mom tried to make me bus tables." She spread her legs, extracted the wedge from her crotch with her thumb and forefinger, and started walking toward the furnace ruin. "I said 'Sure, sure I'll work for Dwayne's sorry ass' and then walked back to the kitchen and straight out the door! Mom ran out to the barn when she heard me trying to start the bike and the damn thing wouldn't start till she was about two inches away so I popped a wheelie across the parking lot with her yelling, 'You get back, you get back!' like once I'm rolling I'm gonna stop because she's telling me to. And Buck's up on the steps with these other jerks just laughing their asses off. I guess it was pretty funny."

At the foot of the furnace ruin, she pulled onto the face of the quarried blocks. She always had a plan, a loose agenda from which to work. This was not conniving so much, Reed believed, as it was just the natural way she operated. She took control, Reed thought at the time, because it was the best way to get what she wanted.

"This is where you bring the Climb Club to practice, isn't it? The chalk kind of shows the way, huh? Look, I'm as tall as you." She made a move. "Now I'm taller. And this is where the chalk thins out. This is where it gets really hard, right?" She made a move, surprisingly technical, and advanced farther up the rock. "But it's not really."

Her hips jutted out. Manners should have made him step back, but his mind staggered at the possibility that this…*this*…was what she meant to offer. He looked up at her. This was no invitation. This was a demand.

FINGERS AS HOOKS, legs pushing up and out, elbows locked, letting his bones carry his weight, he pulls himself onto the concave surface of the overhang. Move fast. Calmly. Rhythmically. Deliberately. Conserve strength. Hang on straight arms. Keep feet pushing into the rock.

Grit falls in his eyes, burning like salt. Blinking and flinching, the impulse is to put his hand to his eye. He forces his eyes open and pulls his shoulders onto the vertical surface, legs swinging over seventy-eight feet of air. Swing once. Swing twice. The third time he makes the reach for the chicken neck with his left hand. His grasp is not what it should be but he has a pinch. He pushes up with the palm of his right hand and swings his knee onto the surface. His left hand closes on the neck. Through the blear of tears he searches for the next hold, locking onto it with his eyes, holding it there in his vision, pushing himself up with his legs, finding the hold not to be a grip, but another pinch, a momentary purchase between fingers and thumb. Not a place to rest, he pushes out against rock and gets his free hand swinging up before his eyes have even found a target, working with momentum. A Hail Mary slap finds a sandstone flake. Left handed pull-up, aided by whatever leverage his toes can find. The sandstone holds. He jams the fingers of his right hand into the three-inch crack, pressing one surface of the rock with his fingertips, the opposite surface with his knuckles. Up, up and away. No reason to even consider the pain.

Boulders had been leveraged into position at the mouth of the shelter in the mid-1600s. A reach-around grasp on one of these rocks is his last move before pulling himself into the shelter, face and belly in the dirt like a snake. He rolls over and over, coating himself with sand and earth and the ashes from ancient campfires.

The thing he did at the furnace ruin took him by surprise. Surprise not only that he would or even could, but that he enjoyed such a thing so thoroughly. No. Enjoy was too weak of a word for it. Too secular. What happened at the furnace ruin was nothing less than a revelation. In that moment he knew how empty he had become, how void of self-definition. Now he knew who he was. He was the man, the creature some would say, who does this thing for April Jackson. The man who cherishes the act. Yes, April was a necessary part of the definition. Whatever this feeling is, April is its sole proprietor.

"If the world knew…" Reed said in the shade of the furnace ruin, and left the sentence unfinished.

"The world would be jealous," April had said, lying beside him.

He stands and looks to the rocks below. A wind sets tons of cedar crackling. He hadn't fallen. He wouldn't jump. So he will climb down. The easy way. On the arrete.

The arrete is a good feature of the climb, a trap door, a handy way out if things get bad. Descending like a ladder, he occasionally kicks out a loose stone but stays connected to rock with at least one hand or foot. Though the ground is lost in darkness, he knows he is only feet from the base, twenty at most. He has it made. He's home free.

Then

he

falls.

FALLING IS THE FUN of climbing, the exhilaration of unexpected flight. Of the billions of humans on earth, how many of them are moving through the air in a singular relationship with gravity at any given time? The percentage had to be infinitesimal, and Reed always caught a spark of the divine whenever he was catching air. Only once had an anchor popped, and then the next one in line had held fast.

There is no danger of an anchor popping now. Still, he finds himself strangely serene as he falls. He reaches out and lets his palms scrape the rock, pulling himself in, getting his forearms onto the stone and hugging it to his chest. His knees make contact. Fabric and flesh around his thighs rip. Then his feet are suddenly impacted and he goes down on his butt and into a back-roll, coming to rest face down in the sand by the stream, spit out like Jonah from the belly of the whale.

He takes inventory. Fingers, toes, hands, feet, and on through all the articulated joints. Nothing broken, but the nail was ripped off his right middle finger and his left knee has taken a hell of a wallop. But he can walk, so he can make it to his truck.

Reed McCampbell finds his pack and changes his shoes. A nearly full moon is rising, touching the overhang and undoubtedly peering into the shelter, though that is hidden from view. Truth comes with blows. He had read that somewhere. And now, limping and bleeding, he was in possession of a reality.

He will stop this stupidity. He will leave Kentucky and April Jackson. There will be no other like her in his future just as there was not one like her in his past. He will move on to California or the Gulf Coast. Get away from winter. Get away from April. Though both his finger and knee throbs in equal measure, he will forget about the pain, drive it underground, live through the present with a better future in mind. That's the way. One step in front of the other. The ache in his chest or the pain shooting down his calf will not last forever.

The aspirin bottle in the first aid kit he keeps in his truck contains only two pills. That'll have to do. He washes the tablets down with canteen water, then pours what dust there is in the aspirin bottle onto his tongue. There're the coins she had rolled. She had put them in a paper bag and tied them with a fluorescent orange shoestring and now he carries them on the floor of his truck, a source of a twinge every time he sees them. He has an impulse to throw the bag out on the side of the road, but thinks better of it. He rips open an antiseptic wet towel and tries to wipe the grit and dried blood from the abrasions on his arms and legs, but succeeds only in opening the wounds again. They aren't deep, but they're wide.

He drives west on the Mountain Parkway. He'll stop this foolishness. Never mention the incident. Forget about April. Forget about her altogether. That will be his mantra. That girl is history, he tells himself as the pain swells.

At the Stanton interchange he pulls off the Parkway and finds a Kroger's. Tylenol PM will do the trick. A good night's sleep and he'll wake up sore as hell and mail his letter of resignation to the school board. Then the die will be cast. His course set.

The customers at the check-out counters stare as Reed limps through the automatic door, covered in blood, his T-shirt torn, his shorts ripped to the crotch. In the clear light of the supermarket, he sees that the antiseptic wipes only smeared the grit and grime into a gory mix.

"Mommy!" a child shouts from her seat in the shopping cart, pointing her chubby little finger. An elderly man ducks down the paperware aisle.

Reed finds the Tylenol and picks up a cold bottle of California wine. Just what the doctor ordered. In the fall, he will start a new life out west. No. He's starting it *now*. The check out girl acts like she doesn't want to take his money, and when she makes change, she lays it on the counter.

"What are you looking at?" Reed grunts at the bag boy. If people don't know what he's been through, that's not his fault. The first thing to catch his eye as he opens his truck door is the fluorescent string around the bag of coins. Isn't there a machine in Kroger's that exchanges coins for cash? He'll get this bag of memories out of his life in short order. He scoops up the coins and heads back to the store.

Through the plate glass, customers and employees have been watching his agonized march across the parking lot. Now, several customers visibly recoil at his Second Coming. The bag boy goes to find the manager, who arrives on the scene just as Reed clears the automatic door, hobbling like some peg-legged pirate with a treasure in need of rapid burial. Every beat of the Muzak can be heard. *We've only just begun...*

So he is to have an audience. Fine. Such a turning point in one's life needs to be witnessed. He plops the bag down atop the coin changer with a flourish. Not bothering with the string, he rips the plastic and dumps the rolls onto the top of the coin machine, loosening, dozens, then hundreds, then a thousand, tiny yellow hearts.

STDs

STDs

My name is Pearl and this is my 1000 word report on STDs given to me by Judge Snavely of the Ross County Juvenile Court. If I look a certain way at this screen I can see a reflection of whats going on behind me and this is a place where it might really pay to watch your back if you know what I mean. Ive only been here a little while and Ive decided to stay out of trouble for once.

Anyway. This old hippy who works here (Shasta Ossenburger Child Care Worker IV (Nasty Shasty!!!)) has this girl Shaneeka and this boy Jamal in the Infirmary and there eating cookies and dancing to Two-Pack Chancre or someone whose real pissed about being a rich recording artist and wants to pop de cap! pop de cap! while I set here acting like Im writing this report listening to this stoneage computer crank and grind and try to connect to IronHorse.com. Crank. Crank. Crank. Come on compu. Connect me to my baby!!!

Old Ossenburger dances like shes about to O.D. on dumbass pills. Grinning like an Idiot. Putting her hands together like shes showing a retard how to shape a hamburger. The old gals wearing the same brand of sandals Moses mustve worn and Oh God now shes shaking her disgusting butt. Now its Blind Willie Watermelon or someone singing about waking up with shackles on his feet. God. I feel sorry for Jamal cause he seems like a cool guy and I can tell hes embarrassed but hey you gotta use what you got so shake that thang Jamal!

Word Count says I got 292 words but I dont even have that many cause I cant use the stuff about the dancing so I highlight the first sentence an come up with 29 words witch is pretty depressing. But the good news is I got through to IronHorse.com and if you want to know the truth

Ive decided not to hang around this place long enough to finish this fucking report anyway.

I minimize Word and go into the document source of IronHorse.com with the password and leave a message in the first code line for JD Vogelpohl: U THERE? Though I know hes not yet. Hes still locked up for using a miner in sexually explicit material. Except he didnt do it. It was like I told the judge. JD was running a Tilt-a-Whirl in Tazewell Tennessee when that picture went up and as soon as the guy who runs the carnival is found JD and the rest of the Iron Horsemen will get out of jail.

Shit. Shaneeka. Click. No more IronHorse.com.

Wut you doin? she inquires in a low farty voice. The dancings over and she just took a bag of Combos from this little twerp named Jeffery.

Hi Shaneeka, I reply cheerfully. Im just working on this darn report.

Poor old Shaneeka (eeka! eeka!! eeka!!!). Shes got the eyes of an ape whos been cruelly tricked again and again. Here Miss Ape. Open this box for a bag of Combos. And she opens the box and a big fist on the end of a spring smacks her in the kisser.

Here Miss Ape. Open this *other* box for a bag of Combos.

Duh hell you say! she farts.

Very well then Miss Ape. I shall open the box myself. Oh looky! A big-ass bag of Combos! To bad you didnt open the box. Now theyll just have to go to someone more deserving. Someone willing to take a risk for the things they want.

Hey gimme dem Combos!

Sorry. No can do. But heres another box——

Poor old stupid Shaneeka.

Wut you *really* doin? she grunts.

Planning my getaway Crack Baby! (course I dont *really* say that). Im just working on my report, I answer brightly. Look. Heres the picture Im using for the cover page. And I show her this downloaded photo of a big rotten pecker. Yummy huh?

You *shit*, Shaneeka says spraying combo spits.

Sure I shit Shaneeka. Dont you?

Im just trying to make conversation but she reaches out and pinches my arm.

YOOWWW!!! Whatd you do that for you fuckugly ape?

Well thats sure the wrong thing to say. She grabs my hair and slings me halfway across the room. Ms. Ossenburger does a fast disappearance and all the kids start laughing cause Im hurt and I start crying. It was all bottled up inside me anyway from the stuff my foster parents told the judge and the more I cry the more they laugh. So I just tell them how it is. How there just Throwaway kids cause no one wants them but how Ive got this guy named JD Vogelpohl who worships the ground I walk on and thinks I hung the moon and is gonna bust me out as soon as he gets out hisself and how the difference between me an them is that somebody *loves* me more then life itself and thinks Im worth my weight in diamonds.

Well they get a good hoot out of that and by this time Ms Ossenburger reappears with Mr Birdsell (Child Care Worker I) who takes me to the Timeout room and tries to put his finger in me but I put up a fight cause Im saving all that stuff for JD. But Birdsell says I shouldnt even think about telling anyone cause no one is going to believe me anyway after all the shit Ive pulled.

STDs

Hi! My name is Pearl Jackson an this is my 1000 word report on the Sexually Transmitted Diseases given to me by Judge Donald Snavely of the Ross County Court of Juvenile Justice of the Great State o' Kentucky!

Anyway. Me and JD both grew up in Massieville so I saw him around but never talked to him cause my father and his father were the best of friends who became the worst of enemies after my father stole his fathers wife (my mom) who was the most exotic woman in all of Massieville. So once Dad and Mom and me were in the truck and we were at the crossroads when JD and his dad rode up. JDs dad was moving his lips and though I couldnt here what he was saying I didnt have to guess since my dad was laying down what was probably a pretty fair translation and my mom was weeping and wailing about the shattered hopes and broken dreams shed left in her wake. We turned so that I passed right by JD who was already in high school and he took his finger and stirred the air next to his head so I stirred the air next to my head to and we laughed.

The first time we really talked was after mom and dad died and our place was being auctioned and I was in the barn cause Lucky had pups. I was eleven and JDd just graduated so we played with the pups and listened to the auctioneers voice and every once in awhile his Dad who was laughing and buying things and making comments.

Im ashamed of him, JD said. Hes been drunk since he heard. He loved her so much and it just got twisted around like this.

He said he had to go and when I looked up he was looking down and I never wanted to hold anyone like I wanted to hold JD Vogelpohl.

The next I herd hed joined the Marines and knew how to kill people 27 different ways. I was taken in by Myrtle and Morris who set about to save my sole by making me sit on my ass at the Massieville House of the Lord and recite memory verses. John 3 16 and the 23rd Song.

Yay tho I walk thru the valley of the shadow I will think of JD.

And wait for his return.

And when he did this slut tried to steal him from me.

I dont know what happened to Lucky and her pups. I asked but no one would tell.

STDs

Hi! My name is Pearl Jackson an this is my 1000 word report on the Sexually Transmitted Diseases given to me by the honorable Judge Donald Snavely of the Ross County Court of Juvenile Justice of the Great State o' Kentucky!

Im baaack! Not that youd know Ive been gone but Ive been in Timeout *two whole days*! No one here can remember when anyone had Timeout for *two whole days*! See I figured Shaneeka would start some shit that first night in the dorm and it wasnt long before she did. Pinching people. Its a little game her and her posse play where your supposed to lay there and take it. So here comes old Shaneeka waddling in my direction after already making 2 girls cry and Im just acting like Im asleep and all unawares and I let her come right up on me and just as shes about to pinch I grab her finger an shove it back like old Richard Petty downshifting into a pit stop. She lets out a squall and I stick my fingers in her fucking eyes and pump her good in the gut with my knee and pop her with my fist any place I can backing her up and staying in her face the whole way when all of a sudden the stupid shit hits the deck like a load of lead.

Oh poor Shaneeka! (Bad break bitch.)

Its Super Bowl time an Pearl is kicking off from the fifty-yard line with Shaneeka receiving! Drum roll please! Aaannnnddd *BOOM!* Pearl sure did give the old pigskin a boot didnt she Al? You got that right John! That little chick can flatout *kick!* and *kick!* and *kick!* The fucking fans are going *crazy* as she just keeps those blows coming! POW to the gut! BAM to the back! SMACK to the big fat ass! Pearl comes down on her right foot and fires with her left this time. What technique! What style! POW to the big fat neck! SMACK to the big blubbery mouth! What a crowd pleaser! Then yellow flags are down all over the field as Ossenburger and Birdsell come running into the dorm! And you keep your finger to yourself this time you fat fuck! Pearl screams as Birdsell carries her away still fighting like a wildcat!

So I was in Timeout until they let me out this morning. It wasnt bad. They brought me food and took me to the john when I banged on the door and whenever they did Id shoot a stare to Shaneeka like I was gonna kick her ass again. Then when I was walking down the hall to breakfast this morning this little black chick who bounces her head like a bobble dog came up an gave me five an sez wazup dawg? Shaneeka was up ahead so I said Shaneeka eeka! eeka!! and gave her the finger when she turned around. Then Latisha (the bobble girl) said it too and Shaneeka said you watch it bitch but we just laughed.

STDs

HOW DO YOU do? My name is Pearl May Jackson and this is my 1000 word report on STDs given to me by the most honorable Judge Donald Tanonald Snavely of the Ross County Juvenile Court of the great state of Kentucky, including the clap, the crabs, the black sif, AIDs, and the green drippy droolies.

God I hate Ms Ossenburger. She took away my snack tonight cause what I said in group. And shes the one always just *beg*-ging someone to say something.

We must heal the wounds that have been opened, she said in a phony high-toned fashion. Whod like to start?

So Shaneeka raises her big puffy hand like its filled with helium or something.

Yes Shah-*NEEK*-kah? Ossenburger says with the sounds real crisp like shes speaking Swahili and its her fucking native tongue or something. Yes Shah-*NEEK*-kah?

Peeple nee sho mo spect, Shaneeka grunts like shes taking her first dump in 30 days and looks at me her eyes still so swelled she looks like a fucking Chinaman.

Hmmmmm. Ms Osteoporosis says nodding thoughtfully as though Shaneeka isnt a total shithead at all but really about on the level of Bill Gates. Hmmmmm. Thats a really great point. Would anyone like to respond to that? and she looks at me.

Mebbee, says I, if Shah-NEEK-kah sho mo spec Shah-NEEK-kah git mo spec.

I was being In-sen-sitive. So I got my snack taken away.

Shit. Birdy. Minimize maximize.

Watcha doin? Birdy says. He weighs about fivehundred fucking pounds.

Oh hi Mr Birdsell. Im just working on this darn report.

Hes the most disgusting person Ive ever seen with teeth the color of asparagus pee. He puts his hands on my shoulders and starts giving me a little massage action.

Its ashame they gonna cut all this purdy hair, he says in an illiterate manner. Maybe I kin get a lock. They jes gonna throw it away enyway an Id lack to hev a lock of yer hair bein yer so famous in all an bein that thats as close as someone lack me is eber gonna get to someone lack yew. And then he strokes my hair and my skin is about to just crawl off my fucking bones and go hide in a rat hole. Its really easy to find yer pictures on the Internet, he says with breath gross enough to gag a maggot. You caint find em here if thats what yer lookin fur cause we got the NetNanny but I was lookin at em jes this mornin at the liberry. I really lack the one with yer feet on the desk.

(Yes. That one *does* seem to be the choice of perverts world wide.)

Ossenburger looks out and says hey whats going on? and looks at *me*.

Oh hi Ms Ossenburger. Mr Birdsell was just telling me about his genital warts. Thanks Mr Birdsell. If I need more info Ill call and he goes away looking like Id been cruel or something.

Minimize maximize.

Either JD is still in jail or hes not talking to me. U STILL PISSED? I type.

So JD went to the Marines and I went to Myrtle and Morris where they made me read the Bible and tried to teach me to walk in the Way of the Lord.

And when JD came out of the Marines he dwelled amongst the Iron

44

Horsemen in a house by the river where in the cool of the evening he went fishing in his boat and saw a maiden sitting in the boughs of a sickamore tree where it did overarched the water and she was beautiful beyond compare.

Id herd he was back and I was in that tree on purpose.

Whatre you reading, he asked paddling against the current just to stay in place.

Words, I said and kept my eyes on the book. (I was playing my Long Game see.)

You remember me?

I looked at him like he was a bother. Somehow hed managed to get even better looking. No, I said. I dont think so.

Dont lie, he said. I bought a bike that didnt run but now it does.

Thats great JD, I said like it was the boringest thing in the world.

Well I was thinking, he said. Ive started a web site and put pictures of guys and there bikes an alot of guys have there girlfriends in the picture and there hasnt been a girl on my bike yet. Not since it started running again and I saw you out here the other day and I couldnt believe how very beautiful youve become. Well I thought youd sure make that bike look good. Hell youd make a Honda look good.

I should tell you, I responded in a superior way, that aunt Myrtle told me not to speak to you. Ever.

Oh, he said and slacked off paddling so that the canoe drifted a little.

But what she dont know, I said, she dont seem to mind. (Long Game over.)

So I started going over to the house on the river and JD road me around on backroads and let me help build this website called IronHorse.com witch was about the club and the rides they went on and had lots of pictures of bikes an there were several shots of JDs bike with yours truly on it. Mostly he treated me like a little kid but every once in awhile Id catch him looking at me another way and I knew thats what I had to work with. Anyway. At night the Horsemen had these bonfires I couldnt go to but I could set in the backyard and see the firelight in the trees and here the music and wonder what JD was up to. It wasnt hard to imagine. Barb the slut was always bending over to give him a jug shot. She did it right in front of me too like everyone didnt know we were just waiting around til I got a little older.

Then they started planning this ride to Florida and all I herd was Pearl you cant go. Pearl your to young. Pearl youve got school. And when they left sure enough that fat cow had her tits smashed up against JDs back. So I cried till I got tired of it. Then I hatched a plan.

JD is nuts about the website see. Hes always changing things and checking in to see how many visitors have been there. He almost cant pass a library without stopping to check on the web site. So while the Horsemen were on there way to Florida I would go to the house by the river take the key from the fake rock under the step and go in and post pictures of myself on the website. Just to get a rise out of JD. They werent nothing at first. But guys started emailing suggesting that I set this way or that. Or unbutton this button or that. Then another site linked on that was linked to all these other sites and I had a regular fan club. All except JD who was keeping mum. Whats his story? I wondered. To busy with Barb? The next time I logged on all my pictures had been taken down and my fans had been blocked from email. But what really pissed me off was that he didnt leave a message. No Wish you were here Pearl or Miss you bunches. Thats when I posted that other picture and thats when the viagra Niagara hit the fan! There were *hundreds* of emails and *thousands* of hits on the site! It was unfuckingbelievable! And even after JD took the site down that picture kept cropping up other places. It just kept marching on like that broom Mickey Mouse chopped up. It even got on that show CrimeWatchUSA but with my head cut off and little blurry spots over my boobs.

Anyway. JD emailed that I neednt do any more and that he was on his way home and that we needed to talk witch was what Id been saying all along. Then his transmission broke and he took that Tilt-a-Whirl job in Tazewell Tennessee.

Sexually Transmitted Dis-ease

How do you do? My name is Pearl Sue Jackson and Im fourteen years old and this is a one thousand word report concerning the really disgusting an truly sickening topic of STDs (Sexually Transmitted Dis-eases!) witch was given to me by none other than the most honorable Judge Donald Tononald Shenonald of the Ross County Juvenile Court of the Commonwealth of Kentucky! It is my sincere hope and dream that after reading this if you ever see a boys pecker again you will run in the opposite direction as fast as you can! I know I will!!!

Crank. Crank. Crank. Come on compu! Work it on out!

Big news. After dinner the cops bring in this kid named Ricky and Birdy doesnt want to take him. Birdy wont even touch the papers the policeman tries to hand him. No no, Birdy protests in a week and cowardly way. Were not set up fer enythang lack this. Im the only man yere an were over cap already.

But the cops keep saying Ricky'll be housed with adults as soon as hes charged as an adult but Birdy keeps leaning away from that paper like its a copperhead coiled and ready to strike. Then old Ossie comes out and says sure sure well take Ricky. Hi Ricky! Welcome to Juvy Ricky! I herd about you on the radio coming in to work Ricky! Have you eaten yet Ricky? Ricky! Ricky!! Ricky!!!

Well right away old Ricky-ticky-tavy starts giving me the eye like were long lost friends (witch were not). Then the cops leave and Birdy herds us outside into the cage where theres a basketball hoop but I just set against the fence with the other girls cause when I try to play ball the boys feel me off witch is ashame cause Im really a good player. Well right away Ricky pushes that little twerp Jeffery down and looks over at me like hed just sunk a threepointer or something. Then he grabs the ball and starts running around without dribbling like hes playing football and whats funny is all the other boys fall right in with him and start tackling each other and such. Then Ricky starts chinning himself on the rim when CLANG! the whole hoop comes down! So he takes a victory lap holding the hoop like its the Nobell Prize for Retards with all the other shitheads running behind him just cheering and holding there fists in the air like there the champions of the world or something. They run all the way around the pen. Birdsell yelling, Set against the wall! Set against the wall! But they run Once. Twice. Three times around the pen. Then Ricky comes over and tries to ram the rim down over my shoulders but I dont fit. Then while Im still tangled in the net he pulls my pants off and goes at it. I try to fight him off but Jeffery the twerp jumps in and holds my arms down and says, Is this what you want me to do Ricky? Is this what you want?

Then Jamal puts his knee into the side of Rickys head good and hard and knocks the sonofabitch offa me. I throw the hoop off my head and try to pull up my pants when Shaneeka puts me in a headlock. Shes hitting me and it just goes on and on until the next thing I know cops are running into the yard with there billy clubs out and beat the hell out of Ricky Jamal

47

and Shaneeka.

Ossenburger runs out yelling, I want answers! I want answers! But everyone is looking at me cause Im hysterical and my nose is bleeding and I dont have any pants on so I just rare back an let em get a good gander.

Ill give you answers you stupid bitch! I say. Ricky Retardo over there tried to rape me. And this big ape, I say pointing to Shaneeka, *LICKED MY PUSSY!!!!*

I knew that would get her going and boy does it ever! She tears away from the officers holding her and I cock my fist back to get in a good one but just as Im about to launch a string of snot shoots out her snout and down she goes. Stun gun is a good name for it cause everyone sure is stunned when Shaneeka lets loose a good loud load of poo in her pants.

Ossenburger (whos been lovingly attending Ricko and is unaware of the delivery of these warm loaves) runs over and cradles Shaneekas head like shes a hero fallen on the field of fucking battle or something. Everyone just backs off and watches Old Ossies face as reality stinks in.

So as Ricky Jamal and Shaneeka got handcuffed Old Ossie ushered me into the Infirmary and said shell be with me in just a minute so I just checked the place out.

It was more of a break room than an Infirmary. Old number three himself was standing in the corner life-size on a pop machine drinking a Coke. The Old Intimidator himself just drinking a Coke. Next to him was a candy machine where the sweet stuff hung on screws that twisted when the right buttons were pushed. And there was a refrigerator a sink a cabinet with a red cross on it and a garbage can with the black collar of a garbage bag hanging out around the top. There was a really gross green couch slick with sandwitch goo and potato chip grease and in the corner was some cheesy poster of a guy who looked like Jerry Garcia without the grin. In fact he looked severely constipated and his beard and hair was all swirled around so it formed the shapes of people who were carrying pitchforks and sledge hammers and looked all pissed like the peasants that paid Dr. Frankenstein a call and I just knew this was Ossies contribution to the daycore.

Finally the old girl came in and it was plain her plan wasnt to doctor me up.

You just dont get it do you? she said.

Dont get what?

She laughed like a jackass showing me all the black fillings of her nastyass teeth. See, she said. You prove my point. You dont have a clue. So let me tell you how it is. The time when people like you ran things is over she said. It took a long time but the people are finally uniting.

Your right Ms Ossenburger, I said. I dont have a clue as to what your saying.

That only revved her up more.

Ricky and Shaneeka will be coming back, she laughed. And the next time they move to serve natural justice well see that there arent so many people around.

I turned to the window. It was just an ordinary ground floor window with a single latch looking out on a parking lot. No alarm seemed to be attached not that I would recognize anything like that if it bit me on the ass. Across the parking lot was the county garage with a couple of guys in oily uniforms loafing around an orange truck with the hood up. Oil was everywhere. It soaked the driveway in front of the garage. Soaked it good and deep so you just knew if you dug through the gravel every shovelfull would keep coming up black and slick with oil that dripped from cars years and years ago. Oil from cars that drove around during the WW (World War) or even when Monica was giving Bill BJs (Blow Jobs). Oil from cars that were in junkyards now or had been squashed into little cubes and melted down and made into Coke cans and other cars that crash on the NASCAR circuit or cars bought by Ross County and brought back to this shithole parking lot to leak even more fucking oil. I could see into the garage and the walls were slimy with oil. The floor was covered with saw-dust and you could tell it was just packed into one big oily sheet that would come up off the floor in big flat slabs. Even the guys loafing around were oily. Oily hair. Oily fingernails. The kind of guys who carry a pint or two around in their pores. And I was feeling real depressed and down. Then I saw in the middle of it all this honeysuckle bush just blooming to beat the band. Blooming by the chain link fence right in the middle of all the oil and trash that had blown up against it. Blooming in *spite* of the shithole it was in as if oil and garbage was just milk an pie to it and that made me ashamed of feeling sorry for myself and for ever doubting JD and I told myself I had to buck up and figure something out so as to help JD get me away from these awful people.

There was a streetlight out there and a surveillance cam and a chain

49

link fence topped with rolls of razorwire. But stuff like that wouldnt stop a guy like JD. Not when hes as crazy in love with someone as JD is with me.

Is that your car? I asked Ms Ossenburger. That little rust bucket with bumper stickers all over it. Save the Whales. Ban the Nukes. No justice no peace no landmines. Thats what your mad about isnt it? I said. That your so old and driving a car like that.

Oh God did she have a conniption then. She starting spewing even more of her pigshit like big words could make up for driving a Suburu.

THERES A MESSAGE FROM JD!!!! (I'm here)

COME AND GET ME NOW! I type. And I fill him in on the details like the street light and the video cam and the fence with razor wire and whatnot.

Now for the really gross part of the plan.

Some of the emails men sent me after I posted that picture were just awful and I dont like to think about it but you gotta use what you got in this world and those emails were something I had. Something that might help me get to a creep like Birdy Birdsell. The thing was I didnt have a hell of a lot of time since it was going to be lights out soon and I really needed to check in with JD to make sure all systems were go. So I went to the restoom and checked out my pants and it was hard to decide what to do cause it seemed like there was just so much room for personal taste there. I mean it was definitely a point of interest among my internet fans more than a few of witch offered money for my pants. But it seemed like some guys expected perfume while others were a lot more earthy. I took them off and stuffed them in my pocket.

Then I started thinking. I thought about school and how I liked to write stories and read books and was good at it and how the teachers would let me read to the rest of the class and how I memorized parts from plays for extra credit and act them out and how I wished I could go back to that and how the Judge said I could if I showed Social Services I was willing to go along with the program and get my life back on track. And for a minute I wondered if maybe the judge wasnt right and if I just stuck it out I could get back to school going to football games and such. And then there was the consideration as to what was I doing to JD. I mean after he picked me up he would be a bonified criminal guilty of some really serious shit. I mean just cause hes head over heels in love with me should I let him do that to himself?

But there was another voice telling me I was stupid to think things could ever be like they were. Birdy and Ossenburger *are* the program this little voice said. And JD is the only one who is going to protect you.

The computer was shut down. Lets get the bean bags in the corner, Ossie yelled.

I stepped up to Birdy and wanted to just puke. I pressed my pants into his hand and when he looked down kind of stunned I let my fingers do the walking to a paper clip on his desk.

2 o clock when everyones asleep, I said. Come and get me.

For the next 5 hours I laid in bed sharpening the end of the paper clip against the bedframe. Watching the hands of the clock move and listening for JDs motorcycle. The key turned in the door and a pie slice of light spread across the floor. Mr Birdsell took me by the arm and pulled me from my bed. The floor was cold under my feet and it bothered me that I didnt have pants on. Like I was more vulnerable or something. JD mustve borrowed someones car.

Yew gonna get it, Birdsell whispered when we were in the infirmary and I could tell by his eyes that he didnt see me at all.

Just hold on a minute, I said. No need for the rough stuff. Youll get whats coming to you and more believe you me but cant we open the window to let some air in (and me out!). Cant we open the window?

Birdy grabbed my wrists and said, Hey whats going on here?

Hey no need to get rough. If you like it stuffy then stuffy it is. Let me just set down here and… But he threw me on the couch and started in right away. So I started caressing his nastyass neck. Found a pulse. And sent Mr Paper Clip into action.

Birdy jumped up screaming and fell back on the table witch folded up around him so that he laid there on his back with his legs and arms moving around like some hairyass bug.

I unlatched the window and tried to raise it but it was painted shut.

Then Birdsells hands are all over me. Between my legs and up my shirt. Around my throat. I keep looking out the window and try to fight back. I try to kick and hit and scream but Mr Birdsell is just to strong and hes telling me how it doesnt matter to him to go to prison cause his own bodys a prison and hes been in it all his life.

Then things start to lose their color except for little flashes of light.

Little stars twinkling like diamonds on the other side of the window. Stars that take on the faces of all those girls who are on TV and milk cartons because they're gone and no one can find them. I know where they are, all those little lost lambs who never got to finish school, or drive a car, or fall in love. They're cut up into these perfect little stars, these little diamonds that make the face of heaven so fine. And somehow this gives me peace. And that's when I stop struggling. I stop struggling not because I want to leave and become a star but because this is all I have left and I don't want to spend it fighting.

Then the whole window turns into a star. A big bright beautiful star taking the light from street lamp and shattering it all up into different colors so pretty and bright but containing J.D.'s face, smashed up against the other side like someone is using him for a battering ram. Then again. J.D.'s face. The third time his head comes right through the star and then his hands and his shoulders and then he pulls himself in and falls on the floor and hits his head on the table. Still it's enough to make Birdy loosen his grip enough for me to catch a breath and bite his hand.

Grabbing a broom, I start poking, trying to back Birdy off of J.D., who pretty much looks dead. I poke and scream like crazy. Screaming for Ms. Ossenburger. Anyone.

She doesn't come, but J.D. gets up and staggers around and then goes running at Birdy with his head down like a bull and hits old Birdy right in breadbasket, doubling him over and driving him up against the refrigerator. Then he starts smacking Birdy's head against the freezer compartment—*blam! blam! blam!*—until he goes limp. Then Ossie shows up and screams.

"Just be quiet and you won't get hurt," J.D. says, but she screams again and J.D. jacks her jaw good.

We tie them together in a folding chair with Ossie sitting on Birdy's lap, going around and around and around them with duck tape, and first aid tape, and strips of gauze, and ace bandages, and anything else we can find in the Infirmary, and the whole time J.D. is not looking at me or saying anything like I'm not even there or like he's mad. Which I can understand in light of the mess I'd caused.

"How's your head?" I ask when Ossie and Birdy are wrapped like mummies, but he doesn't say anything, giving me the silent treatment bigtime. I try to dab the blood on his head a little but he turns away and tries to feed a dollar to the coke machine. I reach into his back pocket for a cigarette and he turns away like he doesn't want me to even touch his butt.

"God," I say. "You'd think I'd done something really awful." And he just keeps trying to feed that dollar to old Dale Earnhardt. "Alright, I *did* do something pretty bad but I didn't mean for it to get so out of hand. I'm sorry, okay? I'm sorry, I'm sorry, I'm sorry. A million billion times I'm sorry. So forgive me. Okay? You forgive me and I'll forgive you. Okay? *Please?*"

The machine still doesn't take his dollar so I open the refrigerator and find a quart of milk and a bag of soft batch cookies and some Ben and Jerry's Cherry Garcia that is just perfectly softened. So we sit down at the broken table and eat the ice cream with plastic spoons and drink the milk out of the carton and it runs down my chin and he turns to me and smiles. He flicks his lighter and lights my cigarette and old Ossie starts making animal sounds. All you can see are her eyes and she's looking at me like I'm killing a baby or something because smoking is about the worst thing a person can possibly do. She looks so funny wrapped up there on top of Birdy I just have to laugh.

"What's the matter, Ms. Ossenburger? Old Birdy getting a stiffy on ya? He ain't puttin' it up the chocolate channel is he?" I look at J.D. and he's laughing.

"I love you," J.D. says, for the first time ever.

"Do you? Do you really?"

"More than life itself," he says. "But now it's time to go."

J.D. carries me across the parking lot and through the hole he has cut in the fence. When we get on his bike we coast to the bottom of the hill before he turns on the key and pops the clutch and makes the old motor cough and groan and come alive.

Then we're riding along the Green River so still and dark and it's just the loneliest road in the world with no one on it and the lights of town fading behind us. J.D. rolls back on the throttle and the big engine throbs, throbs, throbs between my legs and the wind whips all around me, and through my hair, and up my shirt, washing away everything that happened. Everything. Just washing me clean and pure again. Restoring me.

I put my arms around J.D. and feel his heart beating strong and warm and I'm no longer afraid. I smell alfalfa like in the pasture behind our

53

house before my parents died. And I can smell the cedars in our woods. And there's honeysuckle too. The smell of honeysuckle so strong it makes me drunk.

The electric lights are all behind me now and there are so many stars. Who would have guessed there are so many stars? All shining down for me. Turning the road to gold as it climbs the hill going on and on for ever.

Jimmy in the City

"JIMMY?" THE VOICE on the phone says. "This is Dick! How are ya?"

Dick? "Fine," James says. "How are you?"

"Frankly, I've never felt better."

"Great."

The voice is a New Yorker's, but who does he know here? In the fortnight he's been in the city he's talked to but a few people in the bars, mostly married acting single, and he's introduced himself as James, not Jimmy, which is who he had been in Kentucky.

"Say, I'm sorry about splitting so suddenly but the day I quit I was so fed up with those assholes I couldn't stand it a minute longer. You heard what I told Johnson, didn't you? I told him to kiss my ass. You should have seen his face when I said that. I said, 'Kiss my ass you bald sonofabitch!' Did you get my photo cube? There were pictures of my grandmother in it and I would just puke if one of those other assholes got it."

Richard Schlink had sat in front of James for two days before security escorted him to Human Resources, then, a few minutes later, back to his desk to pick up belongings. Schlink tried to make a show of being surly to the guards. "Why don't you get a real job?" he said as he took the coins from his drawer one by one and tossed them into the cardboard box. "Or do you like the taste of your master's white ass?"

As Schlink was carried away by his belt and collar, he managed to twist back toward the photo cube and cry, "Nanna!"

"The girl who took your desk put pictures of her dog in it. I think your grandmother is still in there though. Behind the dog."

"So they hired a chick to replace old Dick. Nice knockers?"

James looks at her. He guesses her knockers are nice. "I guess," James says.

"Well listen buddy, I want to make it up to you for departing so abruptly. You free Tuesday?"

"Tuesday?" James says.

SCHLINK'S TENEMENT IS next to a homeless shelter, a few denizens of which sit on the stoop drinking from a bag.

"Well kiss my grits ain't y'all a sight fo' sore eyes!" Schlink says, bobbing his woolly head into the hall at the top of five flights. James laughs, though he really doesn't want to encourage another attempt at a Kentucky accent.

"Good to see you, Dick," James says, shaking hands.

"Come right on in an' sit a spell, y'all," Schlink says.

A cat scurries into the closet of the studio apartment. The room and everything in it—the dung colored convertible couch, the particle laden shag carpet, the dingy bean bag chair, even the red curtain that drapes the wall opposite the sofa—all exude Schlink's personal scent. Like his voice on the phone, the stench is vaguely familiar.

"Don't look back here," Schlink says, lurching into the kitchenette. "It's a shithole! You like chocolate shakes, don't you?"

"Well, yeah," James says, settling lightly on the convertible. "I brought the photos of your grandmother."

"Great! Throw 'em on the table. I'm going to make you the best goddamn shake you've ever had. Have a donut."

James lays the photos beside the box of donuts. Powdered, glazed, and chocolate. Schlink's grandmother sleeps open-mouthed in a hospital bed with an IV in her arm. There's a battered 9 x 12 envelope on the table, thick with papers. Across the room, next to the red curtain, an easel holds a dry-erase board.

"Where are you working these days, Dick?"

"Fuck work," Schlink shouts over the blender. "I've found a better way to build financial security." He comes back with two sweating glasses. "Yeah, in a month ole Dick will be netting eight hundred a week. And I'm going to do it," he says, opening his hands to the surrounding walls, "working out of the comfort and convenience of my own home. I know you want to hear all about it but hold off on the questions awhile. A really special friend is coming over who knows a hell of a lot more about it than I do.

You'll love him. You're so much alike. Have a donut. I want to hear about you."

"This shake has a unique texture," James says.

"Good, huh? And it's 100% natural, non-dairy and sugar free. Just add water and you have a creamy low-cal shake like this for only pennies a serving."

The phone rings and James takes the occasion to remove a hair from his mouth. He hopes it's the cat's but upon inspection attributes it to Dick.

"Hello... Oh, hello Jason!... What? What? Sure, sure. Sure, Mr. Gold Star Distributor! Gold Star cocksucker is more like it!" Schlink hangs up the phone and hunches for a moment with his back to James. "Jimmy," he says finally, "do you ever feel like you're surrounded by assholes?"

"Well..." James says.

"Look at those pricks you work with," Dick says, turning. "I mean aren't you sick of those asslickers getting ahead while guys like us, guys who really have something to offer, get absolutely nowhere?"

James sloshes his shake.

"Oh don't play coy with me. You know what I mean. Just because we're men doesn't mean we can't share our feelings. You agree with that don't you?"

"Well, sure," James shrugs.

"Me too! And I've decided to do something about it. What say we chuck the shakes and have a *real* drink!" Schlink takes the glasses away. "And you know what was so dumb?" he says from the kitchen. "The answer was under my nose all the time. All I had to do was reach out and grab it." He comes back with gin and two coffee cups. "Jimmy, I'm about to show you something incredible." Schlink removes a pamphlet from the envelope on the coffee table. "Would you look at this bar graph. It shows a five-year growth record of an American corporation. Have you ever seen a steeper rise in profits? Do you know what corporation this graph represents? General Motors? Microsoft? It's number 273 on the Fortune 500! Give up?"

"Give up."

"Well I want to share with you the story of this corporation tonight and show you how it can make the American dream come true for you. Now I know what you're thinking. 'Hey, what the fuck's goin' on? Has old

Dick flipped his lid?' But before we get into that, I want to show you the kind of profits possible using our revolutionary marketing method." Schlink freshens the drinks and steps to the easel. "Now suppose I sponsor you in a dealership," he says, drawing a circle at the top of the board and labeling it 'Jimmy.' "That means you're entitled to buy the entire product line, through me, at an unbelievable discount! Jimmy, if you never sell a single item, becoming a dealer is worth it in that you will have a lifetime supply of household products, vitamins, and health and beauty aids that you will find *simply indispensable*! I can't emphasize that point enough," he raises his cup. "To your health…. But if you persuade just ten others to become dealers"—he gives Jimmy ten legs—"then you become a direct distributor dealing directly with the company and paying me a mere five percent of your profits. After you become a distributor, you make a thousand dollars clear profit off every new dealership you sell, plus five percent of what your recruits make for the lives of their dealerships!" He draws legs from the legs, "plus four percent of everything *their* recruits make," drawing another generation of legs, and another, and another, until 'Jimmy,' like Father Abraham, sits atop a mountain of descendants. James remembers a health teacher producing a similar diagram on the blackboard to show the spread of herpes.

58

"See?" Dick says. "Once you have a few thousand people under you, you've got it licked! It's the American dream come true!"

"What's the name of this corporation?"

"Shuckles," Schlink says.

"Wasn't there something on *Sixty Minutes* about them?"

"Fuck *Sixty Minutes*. You really think people like Corey Feldman would be getting involved if it wasn't on the up and up?"

"Corey's a dealer?"

Dick pours more gin. "It's in this pamphlet here. You have a sharp business sense, Jimmy. That's what I like about you. One of the things. Let me ask you, when your drain gets clogged, what do you do?"

"Call the super?"

"Well suppose you didn't have a super. Suppose you were a homeowner, like most Americans are. You would probably use Drain-O or some similar product, wouldn't you?"

"Yes," James says.

"Well let's just compare Drain-O with the Shuckles product, Gob

Out!" Schlink pulls back the red curtains revealing what must surely be the entire Shuckles product line.

"Shuckles products are undiluted," Schlink says, taking a tray from one of the shelves. On the tray is a bottle of Drain-O, a bottle of Gob Out, and two water glasses with Styrofoam cups in their mouths. "Whereas your Drain-O is good for one or two clogs, this bottle of Gob Out represents a ten year supply. I have four more gallons over there so I'll never worry about a clog again."

James wonders why he just can't get up and leave.

"Here I will pour Mr. Drain-O in the Styrofoam cup and let him work. Give him a head start! Now we'll do the same with Gob Out. What you're about to see, Jimmy, is that not only does Shuckles offer an ingenious marketing plan but has products that are simply indispensable. I don't know how I got along before I became a dealer and was entitled to buy the entire product line at an unbelievable discount. Let me freshen your drink."

I'm too nice, James thinks, holding his cup. I'm just too nice.

"That shake we enjoyed earlier? A Shuckles product. Look Jimbo! The Gob Out has penetrated the Styrofoam! And if you have toddlers you'd have to put the Drain-O up. But this stuff is all natural. Watch this." Schlink pours some Gob Out into his palm and rubs it on his face.

"*Schlink!*"

"It's okay. The stuff is completely natural, synthesized from the nightshade plant. It's harmless. Unless you're a grease ball!"

"Have you done that before?"

"Ha! You should see your face!" Schlink says, his skin taking on a pink glow. "That bastard who was supposed to be here throws it on like fucking aftershave."

"I'm sold," James says, taking out his billfold. "How much is it?"

"What? Why would you want to buy just one bottle when you can get the entire product line at an unbelievable discount?" Schlink's blush would give him the appearance of ruddy healthiness if not for the corkscrewing of his eyebrows.

"I'll have to think about becoming a dealer. But you've sold me on Gob Out. The cap says $17.99." James throws down a twenty. "That'll cover the tax."

"All the other products are just as good. Better! If you ask me it's pretty fucking stupid to buy the products when you can be a dealer and get them at a fraction of the cost, not to mention netting over nine hundred a week operating out of the comfort and convenience of your own home. Don't be an asshole, Jimmy! We could be partners. I'm letting you in on a deal because… because… I…"

The Drain-O breaks through the Styrofoam with a lewd plop. There's a slight blistering around Dick's lips.

"You think I'm a real shithead don't you? Well do you want to know what I think of you, Kentucky boy?"

"Call 911," James says, suddenly feeling the full hit of the booze. "Put your head under the shower until they come." He throws open the door and starts down the stairs, invigorated by his decisiveness. Schlink lunges to the rail behind him. "I was on to your act from the first, *you hillbilly fag!* You hear me, *fag? Jimmy Winter is a fag! Jimmy Winter is a fag!*"

James takes the steps two at a time. He pushes through the front door and finds Dick waiting for him at the window five stories up. *"Jimmy Winter is a fag! Jimmy Winter is a fag!"*

The men on the stoop in front of the homeless shelter take up the chant hilariously. *"Jimmy Winters is a fag! Jimmy Winter is a fag!"*

James' first impulse is the old one: To run. To hide. He feels the familiar buzz rise in his chest, the adrenaline pouring into his veins. Then there is a strange cessation of feeling, a lull, a pause of emotion as if waiting for something to catch up. James can feel it. Something big. Like that moment the East River begins to reverse course with the change of the tide. That moment the river is running neither north nor south, but just standing still, waiting. And as the men laugh and point and chant their insult, James waits. He waits to discover what it is. Then—gradually—it comes over him. Then he knows it, though he almost can't believe it. He knows this is that thing he came to the city to find. It is not the way he imagined he would find it, not in the place he wanted or with the person he had hoped for, but this is it.

James steps into the empty street to embrace the moment. He holds his arms aloft like Charles Lindbergh or Neil Armstrong accepting ticker tape.

Yes. It's been a long journey, but the Eagle has finally landed. He smiles at the homeless men. He accepts their words. He soaks them up and basks in them. He joins his voice to theirs, re-echoing their cries, aiding them. His voice surpasses them in volume and strength. *"Jimmy Winter is a fag! Jimmy Winter is a fag!"* He does this, and the men grow silent and uneasy. They stare at him as though he has broken some rule, has crossed some line of tribal taboo.

"Jimmy Winter is a fag," James cries, stepping toward them, "and *you're a bunch of bums!*"

James sends the gallon bottle of Gob Out flying, arching like an artillery shell. The bottle explodes in the midst of the vagabonds who stagger and stumble and fall over each other on the steps. James shakes with laughter. His eyes stream at their antics. This is the human debris who sought to shame him?

He turns to the window five stories up, but the Shuckles distributor is gone from the sill. *"Jimmy Winter is a fag!"* he shouts triumphantly. "And so is James."

61

Anorexia Machismo

BEFORE THE SMELL of burning toast woke me yesterday, it went up my nose and made me dream about living in a pine forest where all I had to do was hoe a garden and talk to long-departed friends who kept showing up with bottles of wine. As the dream faded I hoed faster, hoping concentration would make it last, but all I accomplished was the uncovering of dead relatives' faces, barking up at me like dogs.

Burning toast is nothing new in our apartment. Pam usually burns it while toiling at one of her morning preparations. Out of a week's worth of toast making she's lucky to eat two slices of bread. As with a lot of other things, I didn't know that until I began staying home all day.

Hearing her come down the hall, I closed my eyes. She crept into the room, took something from a drawer, tiptoed around the bed and laid a kiss on my cheek so light as to be more warm breath than touch. Still I didn't open my eyes until I heard her key turned in the door, locking me in like some treasure the rest of the world envied. I envisioned her standing there, brown hair pulled back in a bun, dressed in a white pantsuit, exuding the kind of clean compassion that must be of great comfort to the old folks at the home.

I've been to the home several times and I don't like it. Pam is never where she's supposed to meet me so I end up having to search her out, taking the grand tour of the place. I feel like holding my breath and I try to keep my eyes on the floor so as not see the inmates lining the halls in their wheelchairs or struggling indecently to rise from bed. I feel guilt for being young, discomfort that life so often culminates in places like that.

I usually find my wife with some poor dried husk confined to—embedded in—what must surely be his deathbed. "Here he is!" she says gleefully. "Here's my fella!" I take the splotched hand and try to decipher the mumbles that I usually interpret as praise for Pam. But sometimes another name is shouted. Then I know a remnant of someone's history is flashing back. Someone is timetripping and I have a role.

Once, when I had a beard, I found Pam with an old gent who raised up when he saw me and cried, "Jesus!" I didn't know what the hell to do. So I held up three fingers like a Boy Scout and backed slowly from the room.

"Not yet, honey," Pam said, patting the old guy's hand.

Death, along with weightlifting, has become my hobby now that I have so much time. There're a lot of books out on the subject, though most are about flying through tunnels and seeing bright lights at the other end. No one ever makes it to the source of the light in these books, but it is generally assumed to be a positive place and not the flames of hell.

Anyway, every year the two most important days of your life go by. One is your birthday, the other your deathday. One you know, the other you don't. Still it's there, clicking off annually like a lap counter, decreasing your span by one. I thought of that myself one day while changing the oil. When I told Pam, she said I should think happier thoughts.

My interest in death began a month or so before I was laid off when I saw a fellow worker have a fatal heart attack. I was the first one to reach him and, alone, heard his last words. "You!" he said, gripping my shirt. "Rob my locker! You do it!" Then he turned real red.

I didn't know him very well. He died early in the shift, so I had time to contemplate his request for several hours before deciding I'd better do it.

So just before the next shift started coming in I knocked off his lock with a sheep's-nose hammer. I think the cigar box full of letters was his main concern. I scanned them quickly and noticed enough "I love yous" to know what I had. I took his wallet to make it look good and wrapped them both up in his towel, which I threw into an ingot mold. The plan worked because for a week afterward, all you heard was, "Oh, ain't it awful?" and, "To think it was somebody who works right here that done it!"

I've since concluded the guy got off easier than most. It was swift and he had me clean up after him. The only thing more he could've asked for was to choose the time and place, a degree of control reserved for suicides.

When I heard Pam leave the parking lot I rolled out of bed and squeezed off fifty pushups. I've been working out strenuously every day since Pam went back on the pill. I no longer need to add bulk or definition but I keep pushing myself anyway, adding more weights and repetitions. I can't stop. Pam calls it anorexia machismo and I think she may be on to something. It seems to be one of the few things I can control.

So I woke up yesterday, did push-ups, made the bed, turned on the TV, loaded Mr. Coffee, dragged my weights out from under the couch and smoked my first cigarette while thinking of death. It was a day like every other, advancing one by one on that inevitable date when my free lunch, my something-for-nothing, my unemployment benefits, run out.

After a few sets of curls, punctuated by standing shoulder shrugs, I wandered over to the sliding-glass door of the balcony. We live in an apartment complex called Armenian Woods. I haven't the slightest idea why it's called that. There's not a tree on the place and unless red brick and floors so wobbly that water sloshes out of glasses when someone walks by are characteristic of Armenia, there's nothing Armenian about it either. Like the immigrant couple who named their twins Syphilis and Gonorrhea, I think someone just liked the sound of the words together.

The view from the balcony revealed nothing more interesting than the ChemiLawn men spraying green dye on the grass. Then Penny called.

"Springer is dumb today," she said.

"Oh, I don't know," I said, checking to see if I had him on. "I think it's kind of interesting."

"Women who breast feed their boyfriends? They're freaks."

"That's why they're on TV."

"I'm out of cigarettes. Got any?"

"Should I come up or are you coming down?" I asked, though I knew the answer already.

"You should come up," she said. She's never been in our apartment. It's some kind of policy with her.

I snuck up the stairs with my coffee pot, avoiding the steps that creak, ducking under Mrs. Roth's peephole because I suspect she spends a great deal of time there. Penny's reasons for asking me to her apartment are no longer as imaginative as they once were. The first time was because a bird was in her bedroom. Before that, our only contact had been in the laundry room, where she remarked that we were the only people home in the D section during the day besides Mrs. Roth, who didn't seem to count. But it wasn't until the bird incident, she armed with a broom, I with an amusement park sombrero, when we fell laughingly over her unmade bed, the scent of her sleep whooshing up like talcum, that I realized I'd found the perfect little friend if I was inclined to commit adultery.

A week later it was her cat, who was having a seizure. I'm sure these were fabricated excuses to get me into her apartment, though it baffles me still how she coaxed the sparrow in or taught the cat to kick and sneeze.

Penny is twenty and doing her best, with mixed results, to strip away every shred of naiveté. My relationship with her is brotherly when she is in a rare confessional mood. More often I'm her partner in such crimes as drinking before noon and cranking up the stereo until Mrs. Roth bangs on her ceiling. I like spending time with her. I like the idea of going to bed with her. I like it that she likes it that I like the idea of going to bed with her, though as of yesterday morning, we had not done this deed.

Dressed in the football jersey she sleeps in, Penny was on the couch painting her toenails. Her blond hair, held together at the top of her head with a rubber band, broke over her forehead like a wave.

"Don't say a word," she said. "Not until I'm finished.... There!" holding out a foot for inspection. "What do you think?" I think her legs are nice. Before I met her, Pam and I saw her diving at the pool and I said as much. "No wonder," Pam said. "She still takes gym class."

Pam knows nothing of my friendship with Penny.

"What color is that?" I said, tossing her a cigarette.

"It's called Deep Purple. You don't like it."

"Do you? I mean, it really is deep."

"An 'in' color this year," she said. "When are you going to take me for a ride on your bike?"

"I don't know," I said. "The tank's empty. I think they're going to take it back this week."

"You said that last week."

"They said they would," I shrugged. "I don't think they want it back. I think they want me to pay for it."

"Shit!" she said, stalking off down the hall.

"You don't have to get mad about it."

"It's not that," she said from the bedroom. "I can't pull it off, that's all. Fix yourself a drink."

Penny has an impressive collection of booze she pilfers from the Howard Johnson's bar where she works. She chooses the liquor for the shape and size of the bottles, which she arranges by size under her glass-topped coffee table.

I was dosing my coffee with Irish Mist when Penny's second incarnation—hair down, tight black chinos and a loose t-shirt tied at the side—strode back into the room with a bottle of nail-polish remover, cigarette stuck in her mouth like the female James Dean she'd give her eye teeth to be.

"So that's what you're talking about," I said as she started removing the polish.

"Can't bring it off," she said. "I mean it's not like *I* can't bring it off. Nobody can. Not in Kentucky. I could in California. That's where I'm going, you know."

"Last week it was Florida."

"So? This week it's California. I'm giving notice tonight. Wanna come along?" She said it as if it were a jaunt to the mall.

"You wouldn't want to break up my marriage, would you?"

"Oh, no," she said, looking up from her toes. "But if you wanted to go, I'd figure your marriage was shot already."

66

WHEN PAM CAME home I was boiling noodles. She started in with, "The funniest thing happened at work today..." which I ignored by feigning interest in whatever was on TV. But when she came to "where were you all day?" it got through like a .44 slug.

"Oh," I said, gathering my thoughts and breath. The risk of contamination is less if you get a lie out in one breath. "I checked on a job at a gas station and went for a jog."

"What did they tell you at the gas station?"

"You know how it is," I said. "The guys laid off before me snapped up those jobs weeks ago."

"Well don't be discouraged. Something will come up. They might still call you back," she said, heading for the bedroom.

"The place has been sold for scrap," I said, though I knew she couldn't hear. "There's no place to call me back to."

During dinner I had the news on. Pam kept up a monologue, but I paid no more attention to her talk than I would a parrot's. That's the way it's been for several months. I think I'm waiting for her to blow up at me. Wanting it. Instead she says, at least once a week, "Do you want to talk about it?" and I wonder just what she thinks *it* is.

I know. *It* is the house we were going to buy, the baby we can't have, our dwindling bank account, and a future that suddenly doesn't look so hot. *It* is my emasculation and the way her going off to work each morning underscores it. I can't imagine why she thinks I would want to talk about *it.*

After dinner I watched TV and Pam went to the extra bedroom, called the den or the sewing room depending on who's in it at the time. She always sews when she's upset. Rag dolls for church bazaars if she doesn't have anything else to do. Her father died not long after we were married and she stayed locked in the sewing room almost around the clock. After a while I heard her crying and finally found the door open. Piled in the corner, made from curtains, sheets and old clothes, were dozens of these crude little dolls. "I'm out of thread," she said.

I remembered that when I knocked on the door. "I've got to get out of here for a while," I said. "That's what's wrong with me. I've got cabin fever. I'm going over to Jim's, drink a few beers, and watch a little HBO."

"Will you call if you're late?" she said from the other side of the door.

I promised I would.

I drove to the Interstate, to the Rum Keg Lounge, nestled conveniently in the Howard Johnson complex between the restaurant and the motor lodge. The Rum Keg is decorated in a sailing-ship motif complemented by plenty of red leatherette and black Formica. Everyone there watches the door. Everyone believes the person who will change his or her life will walk through that door if only he or she waits long enough. Around some of the tables, circled like a wagon train in Indian Territory, sit the girls from the office, mostly married and mutually distrustful of what the others would say if they dared to dance. Next to them, the Weight Watchers, fresh from a meeting and getting giddy fast on empty stomachs and rum-and-Diet Cokes. Salesmen strut polyester, dropping names of the places they've been, like Knoxville and Parkersburg, searching for females to ply with drinks and take back to their color co-ordinated rooms with their sanitized commodes and sauna bulbs. By the end of the evening, most will still be alone, trying their slurred lines on weary barmaids.

But it was early now. The evening was full of promise, the women were full of laughter and the men were gaining confidence and courage with every drink they took.

I found Penny working the bar in a black bodysuit and silver high heels that gave her cheerleader legs an elongated, showgirl look. The men's eyes were fixed on her bottom as she walked back and forth filling orders, their heads moving in unison like they were at a tennis match. When she saw me she smiled and came to my end of the bar, passing several upraised, empty mugs.

"What'll ya have, sailor?"

"A draft," I said.

"Is that all?"

"Let me think about it a while."

She went to the other end of the bar and began drawing beers. I checked my watch and knew what Pam was watching on TV, if she wasn't still sewing.

"Have some water while you make up your mind," Penny said, returning with an iced tumbler. A shaved-headed guy with a cat's-eye pinky ring and matching white patent-leather belt and shoes asked her if she'd like a sauna after work. The men around the bar smiled, visions of glistening sweat on taut, tanned flesh dancing through their heads. I sipped the water and discovered it was vodka or gin. I could never tell the difference. Penny honked a Harpo horn over the bar and winked at me before veering off with the tray of drinks. Everyone at the bar looked at me so—what else?—I flexed.

I talked to a lot of people last night, for it is impossible for me to go anywhere in this town and not know people. And every time I'd turn around there'd be another glass of vodka at my elbow. So I'd put down my empty, pick up my full and swivel on my stool just in time to talk and drink with another familiar face.

"Ah, Penelope," I said, putting my arm around her waist when she finally came out from behind the bar and walked by. She stepped in close between my legs and let me rest my hands on her hips. "Have you met the great Howard Johnson during your employment?"

"That's just a name like Tony Tiger or Betty Crocker," she said. "There's no one really named that. Is there?"

"Of course," I said. "He rides the nation's Interstates in a chauffeur-driven limo with an orange roof. When he get hungry, or sleepy, or has to take a dump, he calls headquarters and tells them to put in a Howard

Johnson's at the next intersection."

Penny giggled. Pam is a bit too big to giggle. Penny, just right.

"Really," I said. "I've read all about it. It's an empire built on the body functions of a little old man in a limo who's wild about ice cream and fried clams." She laughed and kissed me on the cheek.

"Have you given notice yet?" I asked.

"Not yet. The manager is getting drunk in his office and hasn't come out yet."

"If you don't, I shan't speak to you again," I said.

"If I do, you probably shan't speak to me again either."

"Wrong," I said. "I've decided to go with you."

"What?"

"I'm taking my motorcycle and heading west," I said. "With or without you, I'm going."

"Oh, God," she said. "You're drunk."

"Yes, but I made the decision this afternoon."

"Oh, God," she said again. "Are you serious? I just wonder how well you've thought this out."

"Hey, Miss!" the guy in the patent-leather combo yelled. "Could I have a Bud when you're finished?"

She walked to the other side of the bar in a daze. "And I would like that served in your slipper," he said.

"Sure," Penny said vacantly, pulling off her shoe and setting it on the bar as though it were a common request. Penny opened the bottle and the man jumped back from the stream of foam shooting through the open toe like a white snake. "How about you?" she said, putting her other shoe in front of the man on the next stool. "Here" —pouring— "it's on the house." She turned to me and said, "I'll meet you in the parking lot," then padded away.

I WOKE UP early this morning, still drunk in the way that makes the heart speed and the brain take a hurried inventory of what was said and done the night before. Last night, passing my own door behind Penny, I thought I'd finally acted, had finally made a decision that flew in the face of my desperation. Now, waking in my usual bed, I suspected I had betrayed a trust and nothing more.

I watched Pam as she slept. She had aged. Not much and not adversely, but it was there. I watched her and knew that I loved her, knew that love was not the missing element.

The radio alarm clicked on with a Beatles song. Somehow youth had flashed past me without being savored. Innocence had worn away imperceptibly and had not been replaced by wisdom. There was nothing to mark the time. I had made no decisions, taken no risks. My life had proceeded predictably down the path of least resistance with only acts of terror to rivet me to any particular time or place. One day, I knew, I'd be in a bed just like this morning but I'd be dying. Then I'd be able to look over my entire life. The sum total, all there for assessment.

Pamela slapped the clock off and I closed my eyes until I heard her turn on the shower. Then I slipped on my clothes and took the siphon hose from the closet.

In no time I had enough gas from Pam's car to get me and Penny across the river and out of the city. A few splashes more, enough to get us half way to the Mississippi. I kept the flow going until the tank was full and we could be somewhere in Illinois. Then I went back to the apartment in time to rescue Pam's toast.

"I didn't think you'd rise before noon," she said, coming into the kitchen already dressed for work. She buttered the toast and topped it with sugar and cinnamon.

I took a Coke from the refrigerator and drank half of it in a gulp.

"Hot tubes today?" she said. "You never called last night."

"Sorry," I said, walking into the living room, turning on the TV. Willard Scott was standing over a sagging beagle with a can of dog food in his hand. "Candygirl is fifteen," he said. "That's a hundred and nineteen for you and me."

"Come off it, Willard!" I said, switching on *Good Morning America*.

"Today is fish 'n'chips day," Pam said. "I was going to ask you to meet me in the formal gardens for lunch but now I don't know."

"Suit yourself," I said, thumbing through a magazine. She stomped out, slamming the door.

I stood on the balcony and watched her unlock the car. She didn't look up but I waved just the same.

I began stalking about the apartment, looking for something—perhaps some keepsake or personal effect to take with me into the future—but I couldn't think of anything. Then I remembered my rosary, black, with a St. Christopher's medal, but I couldn't find it either, though I emptied all the dresser drawers on the floor.

Then I laughed, wondering how drunk I still was. Then I looked at the phone and listened for steps on the stairs. Then I wondered how drunk I still was.

I lit a cigarette and walked into the living room where another smoldered in an ashtray. I remembered what had been said last night. I wandered from room to room, wondering if I really wanted the phone to ring or steps to sound on the stairs. On a pass through the hall, I snatched my helmet from the closet and ran out of the apartment.

I weaved through the early morning traffic out to the identical box houses of Company Acres. Whole streets had been razed, leaving rows of concrete slabs like derelict launching pads strewn with pieces of shingle and shards of glass.

I turned onto the road that runs past the open hearth where I worked for the better part of a decade. The ends of the building had been knocked out so the cranes and hoists could be removed, giving the building a toothless look. A few of the translucent roof panels had fallen through, leaving gaping wounds. I remembered how sunbeams coming through those panels—some rose, some blue, some yellow—were cut up like a stained glass window by girders. Glittering dust danced in the light while, far below, fire blew through the cracks in the furnace walls and bright red smoke belched from around the doors. It was something to see. It was spiritual in a violent way. The place would've looked like a cathedral if it wasn't so much like hell.

The mill slid by, and I rode through cornfields so alike that the asphalt seemed to move under me like a conveyor belt while I remained in place. I rode the roads Pam and I drove years ago. There was a mist in the air, and dense fog lay in the low spots. An early frost had turned grass blades to silver knives. I was glad to be away from the phone, glad to be where no other sound but the roar of my cycle could be heard.

I rode past names I knew on farm mailboxes, past the tractor path that led to the clover glade where Pam had tearfully initiated my manhood, my body still aching from last night's lust. Gone was such passion for Pam and me. Those wild wakings in the middle of the night that were so unbelievable the next morning would seem almost undignified now. Now we planned sex around TV shows and talked about it as if it were a vegetable.

"Would you like to have sex tonight?" "How do you feel about green beans?" It was better with Penny only because it was novel, something different. I would eventually know her body as well as Pam's, and then what? Head for Hawaii with the woman across the street? Seek eternal excitement with a different partner every night?

A school bus came over a rise, flashing its lights, and stopped in front of a farm lane where a pickup was parked. A little girl scooted across the seat to kiss her father good-by and then scurried across the road. As the bus pulled past me she walked down the row of windows, waving to her dad. Maybe that was the kind of love meant to take up where passion left off.

I wondered where I'd be if I'd done anything but gone into the mill. I recalled some nonsense about becoming a doctor, followed by a brief longing for the sea, but in the end I did the sensible thing and started out at sixteen dollars and twelve cents an hour at the age of eighteen.

Even then someone probably knew the place would close. While people married, had children and took out mortgages, someone decided to take the money and run. The decision might've been the pivotal point of my life and I didn't even know when it was made or really who made it.

I rode slowly, taking the turns I knew less about. A quitter never wins and a winner never quits. When the going gets tough, the tough get going. And I could maybe see it that way if I had taken some risk and lost. There would've at least been honor in that. But I opted for security and asked only a workman's wages in return. And now I was leaving my wife, our marriage a shambles. Some jerk loots the company and ruins my life. Someone we don't even know pulls an accounting sleight of hand and everything we've worked for is down the drain.

I passed a sign welcoming me to Pike County. I pulled into a place that sold gas, beer and shiny globes on bird-bath stands, and called Pam. After my call had been shuttled around and placed on hold for too long, her voice, scratchy and distant, finally came over.

"Did you say 'fish 'n' chips day'?" I asked.

"Sure did," she said.

"What time are you serving?"

"Twelvish. Where are you? You sound like you're calling from another planet."

"Pike County."

"Pike County!"

"Just across the line."

"How are you going to get back by noon?"

"I know a short cut. Listen, I've got to go. I just called to confirm lunch and to say I love you very much."

"I was beginning to wonder," she said.

As I walked back to my bike the phone rang and an old man with several days' beard growth hobbled out, picked up the receiver and listened to the recording. "Hey," he shouted as I slung my leg over the seat, "you owe eighty cents."

"Let 'em come and get it," I said, turning the key.

I SET A MORE direct course, picking up the pace a bit. Rounding a bend, I come upon the ancient bridge, shrouded in fog so that it seemed to end in midspan against a gray stage backdrop not yet painted. I stop and take off my helmet.

The road twists and rises on an embankment to join the darker asphalt of the bridge, which glistens with moisture. Hurrying through fog over strange roads, it would not be unusual for a rider to crash without leaving so much as a mark on the road. No stigma for the survivors. No guilt for them after the fact.

I focus on the abutment hugging the road where it curves onto the bridge, the letters "WPA" inscribed in the concrete. A head-on hit would do it. One clean hit.... One final lie for Pam to believe.... One last blow to pass on to her....

I coast toward the bridge. Though the incline robs momentum, the front tire smacks the abutment like a racquetball and bounces the bike back about a foot. I sit for a long time, just watching the black mark my tire left on the wall grow blurry. On the bridge, the white lines leading into the fog look like a trail of crumbs.

Everyday Epiphanies

FINDING HIMSELF ENGULFED in fire, Gohan remembered how to act. Remembered to bow his head to close the gap between his faceshield and chest. Remembered to drop his lance and back out slowly, moving his feet with care not to trip over his clogs. He remembered not to panic, remembered that this was only an inferno of dust that would end as abruptly as it had ignited. As the flesh on his neck seared, Gohan remembered.

Then the fire was gone, blown out by a column of yellow smoke spewing from the charge hole. Gohan spun and walked stiff legged to the emergency shower, wincing when his skin touched the overheated fabric of his fireproof trousers. His plastic faceshield, soft from the heat, warped as the water washed over it, making the rows of standpipes on either side of the coke ovens grow and shrink, lean toward him then cower away. He watched the column of smoke, thick as grease where it billowed from the oven top, become vague and indefinite as it assimilated into the August haze. When water seeped through the shoulder seams of his coat, he stepped out of the shower. A gossamer curtain of steam rose behind him as he clopped back to the open charge hole, picked up the lance, and yanked the eighty-pound lid into place, abruptly cutting off the smoke.

On the stair landing, Gohan threw off his gear and looked out over the steel mill. The stacks of the open hearth spouted red smoke; the blast furnace belched white. The rail-laden landscape between was dusted with red soot that nurtured nothing but a sparse crop of hissing steam pipes. In an hour, Gohan would be in his street clothes, listening to the radio as he drove to the home to see his mother. He tried to wrap that scene with his mother up in his mind and disconnect the part of his brain that held it. Then, when he was in his truck, and the wind was gushing through the window, that disconnected part would reconnect and it would be as if the two oven cycles that stood between him and the end of the shift hadn't even existed. This was the part of his mind he would live in after he punched out. This was the part he would take to see his mother.

A HALF-HOUR AFTER clocking out with his razor rolled up in his towel, he found his mother parked in the corridor beside the woman she slept next to at night. "That's that," the other woman said, washing her hands with air. "That's that" was all Gohan had ever heard her say.

He wheeled his mother into her room, pulled the curtain, and began lathering her face with soap and water. "Old women try to turn into men," he said taking out his razor, "and when they do, we've got to shave them."

She smiled and rested her dried apple countenance in his hand as he drew the blade over her soft creases. She had been an attractive woman in the big boned, good child-bearer way, and Gohan had made the mistake in his first marriage of choosing a girl because she bore a resemblance. In the early photographs, his mother was a woman acutely aware of her charms, one who always dressed and stood in a way to show the size of her breasts. In Gohan's memory, she was darkly tanned from garden work, making her pale eyes seem even lighter. But it had been her hair that was her greatest conceit — blonde — and she had never cut it because, she said, the Bible was against it, though in the Scripture reading she had forced on him, Gohan had never crossed the exact verse. Her hair was perhaps his earliest memory, his face tented by her fragrant tresses, his fingers tangled in it. It was really a fragment of a memory, cut loose as it was from any other context. At first blush the recollection seemed as meaningless as a fading dream. But like a dream, there was more to it than there seemed to be, something ineffable and profoundly evocative.

Soon after she entered the home, she was given a rather amateur-ish pageboy cut. Complaining at the nurses' station, Gohan was told by a woman who didn't bother to look up from the *People* she was reading that if he had to wash a dozen heads a day he might sing a different tune. The tune he did sing was of such loud and violent pro-

75

fanity that when he finally turned from the desk he was confronted by three warily circling orderlies, each protesting they wanted no trouble.

He patted her face dry and tucked the towel in around the collar of her gown. He wheeled her to the sink and adjusted the faucet to body temperature. He lowered her head into the hollow of the porcelain rim and wetted the hair over her forehead and ears with the cup of his free hand. As she purred like a contented cat, he worked the shampoo in with slow, circular motions then thoroughly rinsed it. He massaged her scalp with the towel and rolled her into the box of squares the sun made on the floor. Turning off the air conditioner, he began combing out her hair.

"How've you been, Mom?"

He hated the disinfectant smell of the place. Hating that smell was perhaps his earliest memory, dating to his first hospitalization for a disease he'd since forgotten. He couldn't sleep and had cried incessantly until she appeared and told him it was okay, that she was there, and would be there when he awoke. She was young then. He would call a woman of that age a girl now.

"Vance?" she said, turning her head and looking rheumily at Gohan. "*Vance!* I knew it wasn't like they said. I knew you would come back. Where have you been so long? Why did you worry me so?"

Gohan smiled and nodded. A stroke had set her mind drifting among the times of her life, regaining people one moment, losing them the next. Gohan had warred against the drifting when she lived in his house. He read a book on senility and began drilling her on the time, the date, the month, and the year. Constant orientation, the book said. He kept score of how many times he had to repeat something or correct her when she called someone by a wrong name.

"How long are you going to keep this up?" his wife had asked one night before they turned off the light. "It's not fair. You know it's not fair. It's not fair to anyone."

Finally, because nothing seemed to help, he let a doctor convince him that the drifting was really a sort of salvation and that his mother would be better off with professional care. Gohan consented, but he had since learned enough about living with the dead to know that it was no kind of salvation. Visiting her, his closest relative, he was often seized by a longing to hear her interpretation of the events they had witnessed together. He wanted to talk about the games they had played when it rained and the tornado they watched move across a field of — what was it? — strawberries? But they were out of each other's reach now, and no amount of striving could bring them together again.

"No!" she said.

Gohan rubbed some moisture into the bridge of his nose and sat down on the bed in front of her. Again, the fear. He wondered if these sudden scares might be flashes of clarity, moments when she remembered where she was and knew the identity of the middle-aged man before her. Whatever the cause, the frights attested that the wandering trip through Mrs. Gohan's personal history was fraught with jolts. He leaned forward and took the frail trellis of a woman in his arms, telling her that it was okay, telling her that he was there.

Gohan drove a little out of his way to pass the Black Jackson Bar and Grill and seeing some cars in the lot he recognized, pulled in.

IN THE KITCHEN, Gohan kissed his wife.

"You've been drinking," she said.

Why did she have to point out the obvious? Why was she compelled to curb his natural tendencies? Why did she see that as her job?

"You don't have to tell me I've been drinking. I know already. I can feel it in my bones."

Pearl, his youngest, was lying on the living room floor watching *Friends*. How was she? She was fine. What did she do today? She went to the pool with Jennifer. Did she have a good time? It was okay. Would she tell him something about it? There wasn't anything to tell.

Gohan picked up the paper and sat in his chair. Under a headline about a bombing in Israel was a photo of people crawling out of the flaming wreckage of a bus. He looked for the name of the photographer whose reaction to burning people was to take their picture, but the credit only read *AP.* Another photo at the bottom of the page showed a bunch of kids playing in an open hydrant. "One way to beat the heat," the caption said. Gohan turned to the sports. As he read, the paper fell like a slowly collapsing tent over his chest.

Pearl's pounding woke him.

"Why don't we get a new TV, Daddy?" she whined.

Gohan watched the machine malfunction — the single eye rolling back and back and back in its wooden socket — and tried to estimate how many hours he had had to work to buy it. In the middle of his calculations, it struck him that nothing, absolutely nothing, he had ever bought had been worth the price he had paid. As Professor Computer asked if he'd ever wanted to learn PowerPoint, Gohan's eyes closed almost involuntarily.

THE LUMINOUS FACE of the clock levitated like a ghost. Gohan knew it wasn't really levitating. It wasn't even the darkness around it that moved. It was all in the attitude he took. It was in the willing suspension of disbelief.

He followed the imperceptible sweep of the minute hand around the floating dial until a paling shade of gray advanced through the curtains and fixed the clock on the bedrock reality that was the dresser he shared with his wife. If he were working, the clock would shriek in a quarter of an hour. But today was Gohan's and the clock's day off. He slipped out of bed and pulled on his pants.

"I'm taking the pigeons out," he whispered, kneeling over his wife, who mumbled and turned over.

He walked through the dark and silent house to the kitchen where he filled a pan with water and lit a fire under it. Out of filters, he lined the plastic drip funnel with a paper towel and spooned the coffee. He went back through the hall and pushed Pearl's door open with gentle taps.

"Squirt," he whispered, whiffing the discordant odor of a tomboy who was finding increasing pleasure in playing at femininity. "Pearl," he said, stepping on clothes and CDs as he approached her outline. "Get up, Pearl," he said, shaking her shoulder with the tips of his fingers. "Let's take the birds out." She moaned and nudged her pillow. Gohan turned on her bedside light and shut the door behind him.

Since the sun was due to blister over the horizon any minute, he hung a burlap bag over the window of the loft. When day broke, the pigeons would evade capture so frantically they would injure their wings against the wire. Before the sun, they would make no move to save themselves. It was in their nature and something that could be counted on. With a faltering flashlight and a wicker crate, he entered the homers' pen and began caging the younger birds.

With the crate nearly full, Gohan cast his light about for birds he might have missed. His beam passed over, then came back to, Eagle, the large grizzle roosting in the corner. After the bird had won several races — which Pearl had elaborately commemorated on the walls of the loft with colored Magic Markers — Gohan began racing him more and betting larger sums on him. Eagle had probably lost twice as much as he had won, but the losses were worth it when he was victorious. Several days after the pigeon had failed to return from a 600-mile race, Gohan found him on the floor of the loft matted and deeply wounded. Usually in such cases, he would've dispatched the bird and buried it in the garbage can before tenderer eyes could see but, for some reason, he left Eagle as he discovered him. To his surprise, the bird humped up in the corner and, with the help of the milk-soaked bread Pearl pushed down his crop, took on the odds one more time.

When he finished loading the crate, Gohan set the crossbar of the trap so the remaining homers could not go out, then he entered the smaller pen where he kept his Birmingham rollers and opened their trap so they could come and go as they pleased. Carrying the crate across the wet grass of the backyard, he noticed Pearl's light was out. He positioned the basket of birds behind the cab of his truck then went into the house to Pearl's room.

"Let's get a move on," he said, leaning through the door. "Up and at 'em."

"Leave me alone," she blurted, flouncing under the sheet.

"We'll have breakfast," he heard himself wheedle.

"No!" she said.

Gohan shoved the door with such force that it rebounded off the wall and hit his shoulder as he entered the room.

"If you're not in my truck in ten minutes you're going to be one sorry young lady!" he shouted.

His wife was sitting up in bed when he came in for his billfold.

"What's gotten into you?" she said.

"I'm taking Pearl with me."

"So I hear. Can't you see she's too old for that stuff?"

"No," Gohan said. "She's not too old and I'm not too old. We're both just the right age."

Minutes later he sat in a lawn chair on the porch and sipped his

79

coffee as a neon glow rimmed the eastern sky. Now he would be cast as the villain, the unreasonable tyrant, the brutal bad guy to pointedly ignore.

A few rollers emerged from the loft and sat on the landing. Gohan looked at his watch and was thinking that he may as well get going when a faint rectangle suddenly projected beneath his daughter's window. To make sure, he stood and craned his neck. He picked a dirt clod out of the flowerbed and threw it against the roof of the loft. The rollers took off in a tight rising spiral over the neighborhood, climbing to fifty feet or more in the cool air before one, then another, began cascading head over feet, plunging spastically earthward to within inches of trees and wires before pulling out the fall and climbing again. Gohan wondered if they enjoyed their acrobatics or if it was just something else in their nature, something they couldn't help but do. Maybe, Gohan thought, watching the birds flaunt their power of flight just as gravity was about to claim them, it is in their nature to enjoy it.

The kitchen door slammed louder than it needed, then the door of his truck. Now the hard part came.

Pearl sat as far away from her father as the cab would allow.

"Hope that door doesn't fly open," he said as they backed out of the driveway. "It's been doing that lately."

She huddled even closer, as if to fall to the side of the road was preferable to what lay in store. Her hair was long and wild, and the only rule she chose to give it was a part down the middle and an elastic thing she called a scrunchy. Gohan tuned in a bluegrass station and yodeled along with Earl Monroe while Pearl looked out the window in silence. Just like him, Gohan knew she always awoke famished. But just like her mother, she would milk hard-to-please for all it was worth.

"How about some pancakes?" Gohan said, pulling into the parking lot of the Black Jackson Bar and Grill. He climbed the steps and held the door open while Pearl moped behind him. When she finally slunk past, the man at the first table made a show of doffing his hat made of knitted yarn and flattened Miller cans. She stared out over the tabletop Melody Maker at the occasional traffic.

"Coffee, Gohan?" the waitress called.

"Two," he said, flashing a V with his fingers.

The Black Jackson Bar and Grill had a dual personality befitting its single clientele. At night the place was a raucous, even brawling, honky-tonk until it closed at two. A half hour after it reopened at five, it smelled more of bacon than booze, and the revelers who had raised the roof several nights before could be seen sedately eating eggs on their way to or from work, their hair still wet from showers.

Gohan glanced over his menu at Pearl. She moodily emptied the sugar dispenser into her coffee then turned to look out the window again. He slipped a couple of quarters into the Melody Maker and pushed the buttons for "Drinkin' Canada Dry." As the song played, he slowly flipped through the metal pages.

"See anything you like?"

The silent treatment.

The waitress stopped to warm their coffee and, as Gohan asked for more sugar, Pearl punched out the remaining two songs.

"Drink as much as you want," he said, raising his mug when the waitress had left with their orders. "It's a bottomless cup at the Black Jackson."

As she dosed her coffee with sugar, Gohan thought he saw a slight melt in her pout.

"What's that man got all those stupid pins in his vest for?" she demanded.

Gohan turned to look. "Those are lures. He's going fishing is my guess."

"Why's he wearing that dumb hat?"

"He's bald," Gohan said, smiling.

"Well he looks like a big queer to me."

"I happen to know he's shorter than me."

"So what's that make you?"

They were quiet until after breakfast was brought.

"This is going to be the first flight for most of these birds," Gohan said. "And a long one too. About sixty crow miles, I figure. We might even have to eat lunch on the road. You wouldn't mind, would you, if we stopped for pizza or a banana split or something?"

She shrugged with studied indifference, grape jelly in the corner of her mouth.

"...AND IT'S LIKE they hal-*lu*-cinate when they go into the blooms because they have *zill*-ions of lenses and can see colors we don't even know about." Pearl, wiggling feet propped on the dashboard, was telling all she knew about bees. "And when they see the flower, they're drawn straight to it, and this little sucker thing sticks out," she said, putting her fist to her mouth and flipping out her index finger, "and sucks up all the nectar. And when a bee finds a flowerbed, he fills up and goes back and does a little dance for the other bees and they can tell by his steps where the flowers are. It's like they use geometry or something."

"How'd you learn so much about bees?"

"Book from the bookmobile," she said, searching the radio dial for a song she liked.

"What made you interested in the first place?"

"'Cause I was so *petrified* of them. I thought if I knew about them, I wouldn't be afraid of them anymore."

"Did it work?"

She hooked her fingers under her toes and drew her knees up under her chin. "No. Well, yeah — kinda. I mean, I don't think they're so gross anymore. But I still don't want them around me, if ya know what I mean. Really they're kinda neat. I mean it wouldn't be such a bad life, being able to fly and all. 'Course they only live a month, but I figure since everything looks bigger to them, time probably seems a lot longer too."

"It's all relative, huh?"

"That's for sure. I have to use the bathroom."

Gohan stopped at the next service station and filled his tank. When Pearl hopped back into the cab she had a bag of M&Ms. He held out his hand and she dropped a single brown pellet in his palm.

"Come on. Shell out."

She picked out two more brown candies, dropped them in his hand, and tossed back several colored ones. "You only get the brown ones," she said.

"The brown ones. Why?"

"Because they look like little rat turds and that's what you deserve for being so mean and cruel. You were a pilot in the air force, weren't you?" She pushed M&Ms through her lips. She had moved closer to the middle of the seat to better control the radio.

"I launched weather balloons in Greenland, and you know it," he said, snapping his fingers in front of her. "Quit holding out."

"But didn't you ride around in planes a lot?" she said, pouring the remaining M&Ms into his palm, all brown.

"Sure," he said.

"What's it like?"

"Sometimes your ears hurt, but it's nice to look down on the clouds. Of the thousands of generations of people who lived before us, we're among the first to be able to do that. Everyone else had to look up at clouds. That makes us different."

"Don't make me different. I've never been."

"Well, you will. And the first time you do, you know who you'll think about?"

"Who?"

"Me. You'll think of your old man."

"What makes you so sure?"

"Just wait and see."

"'Delmer's Cabins in the Pines,'" she read from a dilapidated sign in front of a dozen peeling shacks with ironweeds growing through the windows. "*Swank.* But you weren't in a war," she said, almost accusingly.

"Just because you're in the service doesn't mean you have to be in a war."

"But that's what those things are for, isn't it. Air forces and armies?"

"Well, yeah."

"So, if you weren't in a war you just wasted your time."

"That's one way of looking at it. Not a very good way, but it's one way."

"It's all relative, I always say."

"Your uncle was in a war," Gohan said.

"Don't tell me. Vance, right? Missing in action. If he disappeared before I was born, is he still my uncle?"

"Yes."

"Some people think those guys are still alive, you know. Being kept in cages."

"Those people are dreaming," Gohan said.

They drove until they came to a practice field on the outskirts of a little college town. Gohan dragged the crate to the back of the truck and put the tailgate down.

"Is Eagle flying?" Pearl asked, peering through the wicker bars. "There he is," she said. "Look at how big his nose has got. Can I let 'em loose?"

"That's why you're here." Gohan glanced at his watch, though he knew the birds would easily beat them home if they stopped for lunch.

A flutter of wings fanned their faces when the pigeons broke from the basket and began to circle, feeling for the instinctual urge that would pull them home.

"Where's Eagle?" Pearl asked, hopping up on the tailgate.

"There he is," Gohan said.

"Where?"

"East side of the flock."

"What's the east side?"

"Where the sun is."

"You don't have to be a big grump about it."

"Here. See? The furthest one from us."

"Where?"

"Right there!" he said, putting his arm around her neck and pointing. "See? He's already trying to pull away from the others. See?"

"Yeah," she said slowly. "I see him."

Gohan let his hand brush the tendrils of his daughter's hair and she didn't pull away from him as she often did. He let his fingers sift through her thick locks.

With scant encouragement she leaned into his side.

When I was twelve,

the sheriff of Menifee County gave me some advice. I don't know if it was particularly good advice, but he offered it at a time when no one else knew what to say to me, and in that void his words took hold. It was the summer before I moved to Ohio, the summer my mother tried to break it off with a man named Owen Dodd.

Houses are there now, but on that hot day in my twelfth August it was a fragrant sea of tobacco divided into quarters by a gravel road and a train track. I was supposed to be home taking calls from people wanting to hire Owen, but the phone wasn't ringing, and Owen wasn't around, so I felt safe sailing my bike through those green waters. But when a train shrieked down-valley, I set off for the intersection, standing on pedals, leaning over handlebars, exhilarated with my own speed. A Ford waited at the crossing, then pulled onto the track. I was the first to the wreck. The only one for twenty minutes.

When the deputy sheriff got there he shifted from leg to leg like he was about to run but couldn't decide where. *"What? What're you doing? Jesus! What're you doing?"*

I opened my mouth but the only sound that came out was a gurgling like air through a wet hose.

He pulled me by my shirt.

"Turn around," he said. *"Jesus!* Turn around and put your hands behind your back."

From the cage of the cruiser I watched flies congregate until the sheriff came and covered the bodies with a sheet. Then he squatted on his haunches at the intersection, looking down the tracks in the direction the train had come, then to where the car had rolled. He touched the roadbed, picked a pebble out of it and rolled it between his fingers. Rising as if pushing up on a great weight, he took rubber gloves, paper towels, and a plastic bag from his trunk. He plucked the blue canvas purse from the front seat of the wreck with a nightstick and spread its contents on the hood of the cruiser. Keys on a keychain made in vacation bible school, Kleenex, gum, lipstick, compact, Tampon, a billfold. Driver's license, social security, photographs, a few dollars and some change. He spread it all out on the hood, giving each item a margin of space, inspecting them individually, then as a whole, taking them in like they were pieces of a puzzle, like there was some answer there. Then he put everything back as it was and sealed the purse in the bag.

Then the sheriff came. "Donny's got you cuffed up, huh? He says you can't talk. Get out here and let's take a look." He wiped my mouth and patted my pockets. "What were you doing in there? Trying to help that woman? That's what I think. I think you were trying to help her. Turn around." He unlocked the cuffs. "Let's take a walk," he said. "I think we both need it."

Were leaves swaying in a breeze? Doves on telephone lines? Cicadas singing? I've been through enough Augusts since to suppose all that happened, but I have only a tunnel memory of watching my feet as we walked. From the levee, the whole scene lay before us. The shadows of clouds on tobacco, the ambulance's slow approach, silent, red lights throbbing. Engineers in greasy coveralls waddling like toddlers.

The sheriff lit a cigarette. "Just when you think you've seen it all someone shows you something else. I want you to listen to me, boy. I want you to let me give you some advice. All you saw down there was a bad accident. That's all it was. That's what the report is going to say. I want you to say it. Say 'All I saw was a bad accident.' Go on. Say it. And believe it."

After a couple of tries I got it out.

Then he asked me for my name.

Diaspora

THE PHONE RINGS. The person sleeping next to me stirs.

Please God. No.

Going for the phone I knock over a half-empty plastic cup of something with cigarette butts floating in it.

"Mr. Timberlake?"

It's Heather at the front desk. The floor rolls when I stand. I snatch a pair of briefs and stagger to the bathroom.

"Mr. Timberlake?"

The briefs are several sizes too big. Nausea wells within me. I steady myself over the sink. The moment mounts, then passes.

"Mr. Timberlake?"

"Yes Heather?"

"I can barely hear you," Heather whispers.

"What is it, Heather?"

"The television people was here talking to this guy in the parking lot with a big feather in his hat then they came in and asked me why you rented the Beacon Room to the Sons of Liberty and I told him I didn't know but if you did you had your reasons."

I can't process what she's saying. I can't process the image in the mirror.

"Then, like these calls came in. A Mr. Beaver or something and this other guy. I don't know what you've done this time, Mr. Timberlake, but this other guy said he was going to blow your Gee-Dee head off! Those were his exact words except he really said it. He didn't say Gee-Dee."

"Okay," I say. "I'll be right down."

I have to get some clothes and get through the door without waking this guy. I take a deep breath and almost gag on the taste of my tongue. I'll take a fast trip into the room, gather my clothes, slip them on in the bathroom and get out the door without looking back. I'll go to a room down the hall and take a fast shower. Pull myself together. That's what I'll do. I'll be fast and silent. Get what I need and get out. I put my hand on the doorknob. I won't even look in his direction. One. Two. Three.

"Mornin', Lollipop."

"Oh. Hi."

"Listen to him. *'Oh. Hi.'* I can't believe this is the same guy who was talking last night."

He looks like Seinfeld's friend. What's his name?

"Look," I say, pulling on my pants. "I just got a call. There's a problem. So I've got to be on my way. It was nice meeting you but I've got to get on down the road. The room's all paid for so just show yourself out." I pull on pants, grab socks and slip into loafers.

"You told me you live here," he says. "You said you manage the place."

"Oh," I say. "Well that was a lie." Then I'm out the door.

I left my contacts in the room so the blurry brown skinned housekeeper pushing her cart down the hall might be Maria Mendoza or it might be Jihadha Mustafa.

"Jello Mister Teemberlake," Maria says. "Did anutter brutter come from outta town?"

I'm glad it's Maria. Jihadha seems so judgmental.

"Hello, Maria. Say, have you cleaned this bathroom yet?" Not waiting for an answer I look in and make out the blurry wet towels on the blurry wet floor. "Good. I want to grab a quick shower." I take a towel from her cart and a bar of soap and a bottle of shampoo and two complimentary gourmet coffee filter inserts that I hope aren't decaf.

"Jew don' wanna wake jer brutter huh?" she says.

"Right," I say. I close the door, twist the sauna bulb dial and start to load the single serving Mr. Coffee on the counter. Last night's guest left the filter pad in the brew cup and it doesn't want to come out when I shake it over the wastebasket. Then it does come out, hitting the floor with a lewd plop and bursting at the seams so that coffee grounds spill out like a big brown asterisk. Disjointed memories from the night before swirl like gin in tonic. I think I'm going to be sick again. Leaning my head on the wall over the commode, I position myself, getting ready. The memories sink and rise, some visual, some taking on words. Oh yeah, Lollipop! Yeah! Yeah! Then it comes. A steady stream of hot rumination. I put my arms around the waist of the commode and lower my face into the bowl. Have no fear, Baby. You are in the hands of an experienced man.

There's no sense dwelling on details. How it comes wave after wave—mozzarella jalapeno pepper poppers and masticated nachos—retching up from the deepest depths of my digestive system as though my very intestines are intent on making me taste it all again. No reason to tell how Maria Mendoza comes to the door and knocks, knocks, knocks with her Latin urgency, asking time and time again — *knock, knock, knock* — "Jew okay, Mr. Teemberlake? Jew okay?"

Mr. Coffee is belching steam when I emerge from the shower and I twist the dial of the sauna bulb again and wipe the steam from the mirror, uncovering an image that is only slightly less ghostly than the one there before. I pour half a cup of coffee and cut it with cold tap water. No toothpaste. No brush. No mouthwash. No razor. No comb. I dry off, put on my pants and step into the hall to find the needed items.

"Can I help jew?" Maria says.

"Yeah, maybe I just don't see them. The valet items?"

"Right here. If they snake, they bite jew."

I take what I need to the bathroom. Unwrap the toothbrush, use it, trash it. Unwrap the razor, use it, trash it. Drain the single serving bottle of Scope, trash it. Unwrap the comb, use it, stick it in my pocket.

"Thanks Maria."

"Jew look like a new man."

GUESTS ARE IN the lobby finishing what's left of the continental breakfast. I grab a bear claw and head for the office.

"Good morning Mr. Timberlake!" Heather says. "I'm on TV! They have that Sons of Liberty guy with the feather then they have me on with words under my face. It says 'Heather Collins, company spokesperson.'"

Anyone who looked at her resumé would know she's a fool. But on the day I hired her I was looking at her breasts, never guessing her brain was made of the same tissue.

"Don't say anymore to anyone, Heather. You understand? Just say no comment. Can you do that?"

"No comment."

In the office I stir the mouse. Liberty's March Publishing Company had booked the Beacon Room way back on February 12 and paid with a credit card at the time of booking. Mr. Naipal took the call and entered the reservation at 6:53 p.m. I log onto the web and do a Google search on Liberty's March Publishing.

Please God. No.

I have to call Braintree. I have to call that prick Dever. God how I hate that sonofabitch. But I have to call him. But first I'll have a cigarette.

I have a cigarette and still don't want to call Dever. What I need is a cigarette and a drink. It's too early for the lounge to be open but I look out the window and see Cedric's car in the lot next to mine, so I know he's in the lounge stabbing cherries with little plastic swords or slicing the limes he'll set on the mouths of Corona bottles later.

In the glass-enclosed walkway between the motel and the lounge, the air conditioning lapses seriously and the carpet is stained from water that seeps in whenever there's a big rain. In the winter the walkway gets so cold the saturated carpet freezes — a lawsuit waiting to happen.

Cedric is sitting on a barstool smoking a Kool watching Al Roker talk about the heat wave. Morning glory, he'll say.

"Morning, Glory."

"Morning, Cedric."

Cedric was in the navy for twenty years and has been a bartender for five. He knows a lot, or at least can guess correctly a lot. On any given night there may be smarter people staying at Howard Johnson's but Cedric is the smartest person I have regular access to, and he is the closest thing I have to a friend. In his much larger universe, I am probably not much more than an acquaintance. He's been married to a white woman, a black woman, and a Korean.

"Ready for the big shindig?" he says.

I go behind the bar and mix tomato juice and vodka in equal measure.

"What are you talking about?"

"The Sons of Liberty or the Sons of Bitches or whatever they call themselves. The Grand Puba says there's going to be a rally tonight even if he has to knock the door down." Cedric looks at his watch. "It'll be on when the local news breaks in at the bottom of the hour. Eyewitness 5's got some really great file footage of the Sons marching through some projects in Ohio years ago and they've promoted Heather to company spokesperson."

I come around and sit on the stool next to him. He lights my cigarette and pushes the ashtray in my direction. Katie Couric is interviewing Sarah-Jessica Parker and the camera keeps pulling back for the long shot. Katie's skirt is short but Sarah-Jessica's is shorter. Both dangle open toed high heeled shoes from their crossed, tanned, naked, long, and slender legs.

"For just one night," Cedric says, holding up his little finger, "I'd bite that bastard off at the base."

"Which one?"

"Either one. Doesn't matter."

The local news breaks in and he turns the volume on with his remote and there is the Grand Master of the Sons of Liberty standing in the parking lot in front of the Howard Johnson's sign. My Honda Civic can be seen over his shoulder, the tires flattening into puddles on the asphalt, the windows dusty and rain streaked.

"This'll not stan'," the Grand Master says, the skin around his eyes scrunched angrily. "Thar'll be a rally or a riat tonat. They'll let us in or we'll knock th' doh down." Then Heather comes on to say that the only thing she knows about the Sons of Liberty is that their money is as good as anyone else's. Then some file footage labeled 'Cincinnati, 1991' is played. A much thinner Grand Master and a group of supporters in full plumed regalia are shown marching with flags, surrounded by cops who protect them on all sides from angry black people. In the background, the gray brick of public housing. Then the footage cuts to young black men scuffling with police. Then to other young men running from a 7-11, their arms full of beer and cigarettes. Twinkies and Ho-Hos. Ding Dongs and Little Debbies. Then an aerial view of a fuel pump in front of the 7-11 spewing flame like one of the oil wells Saddam Hussein lit up on his way out of Kuwait.

"Can you believe it?" I say. "Tell me the station is not promoting this guy? Tell me they didn't just hand him better advertising than money can buy?"

K'oyaanisqati bin Abbaca, the pool boy, sticks his head in the door, then withdraws just as quickly.

"Why don't you fire that little bastard?" Cedric says. "All he does is steal things."

"He'll sue me. He said he would sue me the other day when I asked him to empty a garbage can. Besides, it's too soon after the Brenda thing."

Cedric moves to the other side of the bar, opens the cash register and starts bashing roles of coins. He won't talk about Brenda. He warned me about her, and I ignored him. It blew up in my face just like he said it would, and now he won't talk about it.

HEADQUARTERS PUTS ME on hold. Transfers me here. Transfers me there. Trying to find that prick Dever. Finally his secretary comes on and tells me that he has already left for the airport and should be landing in Chillicothe at three where I am to pick him up *on the dot.* She said I was to light up the no vacancy sign and under no circumstances allow any member of the Sons of Liberty on the property. She said that if I were in my office instead of in the bar I would know all about this.

I hang up and walk to the front door of the lobby. The door the Grand Master intends to smash tonight. In the parking lot is Cedric's Chevy, polished and buffed. And beside the Chevy my Civic. I wonder if the battery will still turn the motor over.

"Mr. Timberlake," Heather says. "I know you told me not to say anything, but I just want to tell you that whatever happens here tonight, and whatever happens to you because of it, well, I just want to say I really admire you. It's about time someone stood up to the niggers."

"Heather, have I gotten any calls from Braintree, Massachusetts?"

"Oh yeah. That guy Beaver called and tried to get all huffy-puffy, but I told him you were my boss not him."

"Okay. Listen. Will you go get Beetricia?"

"You want me to just call her instead? There's a phone in Housekeeping. I can just get her on the phone and hand it to you and you can talk to her on the phone and ask her to come up here."

"No. Just go down and get her. I'll watch things while you're gone."

She leaves and I watch the video monitor until she appears walking down the hall toward housekeeping. Then I run tape three in reverse, looking for Seinfeld's chubby buddy. Looking for myself. Soon K'oyaanisqai appears with something stuffed under his shirt, running backwards into a room across the hall from mine. Then his leering face emerges from the door, then pops back in just as I back into view, socks in hand, hair disheveled, belt unbuckled, shirt tail out, backing into that unspeakable room in the herky-jerky gait of a World War I soldier. Then K'oyaanisqai backs out, shutting the door stealthily, backing down the hall, trying first one door, then another, walking backwards in time until he disappears.

The phone rings.

"Ho-Jo Chillicothe," I say.

"To whom am I speaking please?"

"Who may I say is calling?"

"Eyewitness News Team 5."

The voice still speaks as I return the phone to the cradle. I cue the videotape and delete myself from it. Delete George or Newman or whatever the character's name is. Delete K'oyaanisqai as well.

If only it were so easy.

Back on the live monitor, Heather is making her way back to the office with Beetricia lumbering behind her carrying an envelope. I check my watch. Dever will be landing in a couple of hours. I'll send a taxi. As Heather walks under the security camera, I retreat to the office. Heather sticks her head in.

"That woman is *sooo* slow. She is *sooo* fat."

Beetricia shuffles in, envelope in hand, her feet stuck in her sneakers like they're clogs except they aren't clogs. They're just broken down in back because she has bad heels and wears them that way whenever she has to walk down the hall. As she does the laundry in housekeeping she goes barefoot.

"Beetricia, some bad people reserved the Beacon Room under false pretenses and now that we know who they are we aren't going to let them use our facilities."

She looks at the floor sheepishly. She always looks at the floor. "Thas what I sez but some sez you do it as parta de plan. Like de han' in de glove, they sezs."

I admit I don't understand many of the black people who worked for me. And it's more than variant pronunciations and grammatical constructions. It goes beyond idioms and figures of speech. It goes to our very perception of reality. Many of the women in housekeeping see the sinister design of some controlling puppet master in acts that most white people see as nothing but market forces or garden variety stupidity. But for Beetricia and her friends, there is a shadowy "they," an unnamed "them" before whose Machiavellian machinations there is no defense. *They* make sure the crack makes it into the projects. *They* build liquor stores on every corner. *They* pull all the strings from fixing the lottery and every election to spreading AIDS. *We're* just the victims, helpless and hapless. Baffled as to how they foist these maladies on us with such stealth.

I used to think this conspiracy theory was just another way to deflect responsibility for slovenly behavior, or perhaps a passive-aggressive ploy to get under the skins of white people, like pretending O.J. was framed, or changing your name to K'oyaanisqati bin Abbaca. But now I'm starting to come around. Maybe they *are* out there, manipulating and managing at the highest levels. Perhaps they *are* out to get us.

"We're lighting up the No Vacancy sign until this blows over," I tell Beetricia. "And I was just wondering if maybe you and some of the other African-American girls — *women* — might want to take the rest of the day off." She looks at me like I just grew a dick from my forehead. It's because I said African-American. People only say that on TV. "Just as a precaution," I add, trying to clear things up. "For the safety of the Negro members of the staff." *Negro?* I'm getting myself in deeper and I suspect she thinks she's being fired. "With pay of course," I say, but she still looks like she smells a rat. "We'll resume the regular schedule again on Sunday," I say, but she's still unsure. "I can put it in writing if you want." Then I think I'm making too much of it and putting her on edge that way, so I just

93

get to the point. "So that's what we'll do. And I guess we had best include Maria and Jihadha too. So for the safety of our employees, all employees *of color*, we will *temporarily* alter the schedule. Oh, and could you inform your nephew of this change? He seems to be a little hostile to anything I say. It's nothing much. I mean it's understandable."

"K'oyaani not my neppew. Me an' his mamma used to *go* fo sistahs bu' we don' no mo an eben if we di' I's still wooten claim K'oyanni's sorry ass. I tol you not to hire 'im when you di'. I tol you he be nuttin bu' trouble."

"Well," I say, picking up a stack of papers and tapping it to neatness, "be that as it may, I just wanted to touch base and assure you that everything will be back to normal after we get over this rough patch."

She looks at me like I'm speaking another language, then pushes the envelope across the desk to me. "Yo frien lef dis in yo room," she says.

The phone rings and it's that bastard Dever. "I'm calling from the Lear jet," he says. "Are you sure you're not in cahoots with these people?"

THE ONLY OTHER time I met Dever was when Brenda Gipson charged me with sexual harassment. Brenda had just been fired from a dancing job when she applied at Howard Johnson's, and fifteen minutes into our interview she was sitting naked on my desk. Cedric saw her leave and told me she was from a bad seed, from a mixed race clan who lived in the hills and knew not the rule of law. "Surely you've heard of them," Cedric said, and was amazed when I said I hadn't. "No one messes with them. They kill people. Their fathers killed people and their grandfathers killed people. No one knows who they are or where they came from. They were already here fighting the Indians when the first white settlers came. Then they started fighting the settlers. Hell, you've been here longer than I have and you don't know about the Black Jacksons? You oughta get out more."

I didn't care. She was already my altar, my Wailing Wall into whose fragrant creases I whispered my heartfelt prayers. I loved her. I loved everything about her. I loved to watch her talk. Her idiosyncrasies, her obscure figures of speech and quaint gestures all enchanted me, charmed me, touched some desire within for just her backwoods brand of miscegenational exoticism. I got lost in her vagina and in those mulatto green eyes.

First, the cash register was short by fifty dollars, which I made up. Then it came up short again by more. Then she was away from the desk from 1:30 to 2:15 one night, but her car was in the lot. And the next night. And the next.

"What does it matter," she said when it came time to fire her. "In the big scheme of things, up and down the hollar, what does stuff like that really matter?"

The matter was she'd made an audiotape of our lovemaking in which we did considerable role-playing. I was unusually blunt in the specificity of my desires while she played the part of one weakly resistant, then pathetically compliant, "No, Mr Timberlake! Oh, please Mr. Timberlake. *Not that!*" being her most used line. Her slimeball lawyer sent the tape to Braintree, and Dever swooped down to fire me and deliver a load of money to little Ms. Gipson.

Except I'd already started my own video library of her nocturnal wanderings down the halls to various rooms, the occupants of which I also recorded. Confronted with this evidence, and with my own slimeball, Brenda and her lawyer slithered away in separate directions to find their next mark, and Dever fired me just as I deserved.

"Why don't you sue him?" my attorney suggested.

"Sue?" I asked incredulously. "On what grounds?"

He shrugged. "Doesn't matter. Sue Howard Johnson's too. Sue the parent company. Sue them for millions and millions. Sue them for discrimination. Sue them because they uncovered your birth name. Just sue them. They'll offer you a deal to avoid the publicity. What do you have to lose?"

The case never got close to court, and I never got close to any money. But amazingly, I did manage to keep my job.

MY MOTHER REFERRED to it as "the love that dare not speak its name." I must have heard her call it that hundreds of times — maybe thousands — and never wondered what she meant. Then, one winter while driving home from college, a sign along the interstate caught my eye. "XXX Adult!!! Videos!!! Magazines!!! Peeps!!! 40 miles!" I checked my odometer. A few miles more and "Girls!!! Girls!!! Girls!!! Hardcore Girls Do It All For You!!!" So I started counting the exits and when the proper one came up, I pulled over to indulge a healthy interest in heterosexual pornography. Soon after, I found myself being initiated into that anonymous ardor mentioned above.

It started with a perusing of the well-thumbed magazines on the racks, being careful not to meet the gaze of any of the other men in the porn store. Eventually, the canned cacophony of moans and groans lured me to the back room where video booths were lined up against the wall like a row of port-a-johns. Upon choosing a booth, I discovered that large teardrop shaped holes were cut into the walls of these closets so that one could gaze upon his neighbor if so desired, or perhaps even reach through and shake hands. Well when was it not in the heart of man to be curious?

Go on. Turn the page.

THE WATER IS still in the hot tub when I return to my room, gray and cold, and I don't want to put my hand in it, so I take the wooden dowel from the runner of the sliding glass door and pop the drain that way. When the water is gone the bottom of the tub is littered with short, black hairs and I am reminded that most parts of the male body have no attraction to me at all, even when I'm drunk. Nay. Most parts of the male body are right down repulsive, drunk, sober, or stoned out of my head, and I want nothing to do with those parts. I don't want to touch them or even see them. With women it's different. I have a fetish for just about every inch of female flesh, and I take this as evidence that I'm not a real homo. Sex with women is my true avocation. The other thing is just a matter of seeking any port in the storm.

I throw water around the tub to get the hairs moving toward the drain.

Hairs.

I don't even look at the sheets as I strip them from the bed because I know they are littered with hairs. Curly, kinky chest hairs and belly hairs and back hairs. Hairs from the fingers and hairs from the legs. That's what I mean about men. I don't know how women can stand them.

The swimming fish of my screen saver disappear when I touch the keyboard, revealing a message. "I had fun last night. See you again?" I check my email and learn my reputation as an honorable person of high character has brought me to the attention of an exiled Rwandan General who will give me ten million dollars for my assistance in withdrawing his billions from a frozen Sierra Leone bank account. There is nothing from my mother. There hasn't been anything from her for over a month now. We used to talk on the phone until her mind began to meander to the point that she would forget who she was talking to. Email worked better. She had time to marshal her thoughts and her past words were right in front of her so she could look back to them and regain her train of thought when she lost it. Then the emails became disjoint. Run-on and fragmented sentences became common, mistakes the retired English teacher would have never made when her mind was intact. Then the emails became more infrequent. Then they stopped altogether six weeks ago.

"Mrs. Cohen is sometimes lucid for hours at a time," someone self-described as a Senior Social Coordinator wrote me. "But she has lately been battling depression and now shows little interest in using the computers."

My mother had been an enthusiastic teacher, the kind people thought was in the classroom because she wanted to be there, not because her husband was dead and she needed the money to raise her son. But she did love the job. She taught American Literature to 11ᵗʰ graders, and she actually thought those books — *Huck Finn, The Great Gatsby, The Grapes of Wrath* — had the power to transform her students, to wrench them from the cycle of life in the Pennsylvania coal mines, though year after year she watched them march off to the pits like lemmings to the sea, contemptuous of any kind of experience other than the one their parents had known. Contemptuous of that too, really. She was at a loss to understand this embracing of numbness. Though she had lost her parents in the Holocaust and had barely escaped herself, she was optimistic about the future of mankind, even joyful. "This is a most exciting time to be alive," I heard her say time and time again when I took my turn sitting in her classroom. And she would try to interest us with strange lessons about the mythic power of The Odyssey in American Writing — the Log of Chistopher Columbus, the Diary of Meriwether Lewis, Huck and Jim on the Mississippi. And the kids would sit there too cool and too bored to care about anything a middle-aged woman with a suspect accent might have to say.

We made each other uneasy during those years, my mother and I, each aware of, and dissatisfied with, the other's standing and reputation in the school. She wanted to promote me to the higher echelons of the student social classes, and the more she tried the more I wanted her to disappear. Perhaps it was just such an attempt to raise my standing that led her to share her own story in class that winter of my sixteenth year.

No one was interested. No one cared. It was an embarrassment when tears filled her eyes and, though I had heard the story many times before, I acted just like the others. I pretended her recollections made no sense to me, like I'd never heard of Dachau or the Nazis and that her erstwhile explanations were the incomprehensible babbling of a foolish old woman.

I was ashamed that she was my mother and I let her know it. Then I became ashamed of having been ashamed, and I kept that to myself. Years later, the memory of her story has become a kind of silent monument in my mind to a time when the thread of fate thinned so narrowly that my own future existence was nearly extinguished.

I lie down to get rid of my headache and I know I fall asleep because I dream a dream through my mother's eyes:

97

The prisoners had been marching for hours when she noticed the German soldier stealing glimpses of her as he patrolled the periphery. Finally, he spoke in such heavily accented words that she wasn't sure she heard him right.

"Do you understand me?"

She was so surprised she said nothing. Then he came by again.

"Do you understand?"

"Yes," she said.

He walked away, then came back.

"They will kill you," he said.

She looked straight ahead and said nothing and he walked away.

"See the road where it turns into the trees?" he said when he came back. "Watch me. Read my lips. When I say run, run as fast as you can. No matter what happens, run."

She knew he would shoot her. She knew that was the game he played, but when he turned to her there was something in his eyes that made her trust just enough, and as the others marched into the camp, my mother, age eleven, ran into the forest.

The phone rings.

It's that asshole Dever. He tells me he is calling from the Lear jet and as of now I am relieved of duty and have no responsibilities. Then he tells me I should set up a "command and control room" in the office.

"What's that?" I say.

"Donuts and coffee," is the answer.

THE ASSHOLE PULLS up in the cab I sent for him along with the same company lawyer who was with him when he came to pay off Brenda. The company lawyer is short and Dever is tall, but they have both succumbed to the epidemic of obesity that sweeps America. The cabbie pops the trunk and starts unloading luggage, which sprouts handles and wheels under the short lawyer's ministrations. They wear suits and ties and beads of sweat break out on their faces as soon as they get out of the cab. The windows of the lobby are mirrored and I know they can't see me where I stand so I watch their consultations in secret. They would, of course, expect me to step out into the drippingly humid melange of ragweed and paper mill, but I haven't been out in awhile and I see no reason to go now just because these two jerks show up.

Now they're waddling up the sidewalk and it's no wonder the rest of the world hates Americans.

"I wasn't just here, Heather," I say. "Get me?" She gives me the thumbs up and I withdraw to the office.

"Young lady, I want your name and I want it now," Dever says, coming through the door.

"Ex*cuse* me?" Heather says. "I usually don't make it a habit of giving my name to strange men who walk through the door."

"I'm *Stanley Dever*," Dever says. "Stanley Dever from *headquarters*. I believe I spoke with you earlier on the phone while I was flying here on the *Lear jet*."

"I don't care *who* you are. Someone like *you* don't talk to someone like *me* like *that*."

Heather may be dumb but she knows the pecking order. Big boobs trump sweating fat guys any day.

"Young lady, *I could have your job*."

I step out of the office just in time to see Heather remove her nametag and throw it in Dever's face.

"What's going on out here?" I ask.

"This..." Dever starts, but Heather cuts him off.

"I don't have to take this," she says. "Not from anyone, let alone from creeps like *these*." She gestures to them with her open hand and they look at each other. I look at them too, take my time, assess them, and nod my head. Yes, I agree nonverbally. They certainly are despicable samples of humanity.

"Did they make you feel like this is a hostile work environment?"

"Now just hold on," Dever says, but the short lawyer places a hand on his arm and he stops.

"Yeah," Heather says. "That's *exactly* how they made me feel."

Heather grabs her purse and stomps out and I look at the two lawyers for a moment until Dever begins to speak, then I cut him off, intent on holding the high ground.

"Can someone tell me what just happened?" I say, moving so the surveillance camera is peeking over my right shoulder. I look closely at Dever, letting him know I'm inspecting every starburst of broken capillaries on his sagging jowls. Let him know by a glance that he is a grotesque, a particularly fetid specimen of life on this planet. Come on, asshole. Say something. No? Then I must turn to Shorty and inspect his unibrow, inspect the oily hairs jutting straight out over the frame of the glasses, over the clogged pores of the shiny nose.

"We flew in on the *Lear jet*," Dever says, "and we must—" I pick up the phone and begin dialing. "What do you think you're doing?"

"I have to call Mr. Naipal to come in to cover the front desk. What did you say to that girl anyway? Oh. I forgot. You relieved me of any responsibility." And I return the phone to the cradle. "I guess you guys are going to take care of the front desk."

"I see what you're trying to do, *Cohen,* or Timberlake, or whatever your name really is. You're trying to give me rope so I'll hang myself. Well let me tell you something, Mr. *Cohen*." Shorty touches Dever's sleeve again. "At the end of the day someone will be dangling at the end of a rope…"

"Stan," Shorty cautions.

"…but it ain't gonna be Stanley Dever! You just cover the front desk yourself, Mister."

Outside, the cab driver blows his horn. It is then that I notice the two men sitting in the Buick.

DEVER AND SHORTY stand at the plate glass door watching the crowd grow in the parking lot.

"From what I've been able to learn," Sheriff Jackson says, "they do a rally about every other week." Jackson is a dark man with a head like a bullet and he leans against the front desk sipping coffee and talking in my general direction, he and Dever having gotten off on the wrong foot at their introduction. "It's like a little play," the Sheriff says. "Like some strange pageant. They drive hundreds of miles. Put on their show. Start a new chapter, then leave. A few of these new chapters go ahead and get the uniforms and start going around holding rallies themselves. Most groups die on the vine soon after they're founded. But some get pretty nasty. Make anonymous threats. Vandalize cemeteries and such. If there ain't blacks to bully, they'll find an Asian family. Or even a family with a retarded child. It's just a club for creeps. So we're not going to let 'em get a start here. We're going to shut 'em down tonight and they ain't *ever* gonna wanna come back to Menifee County."

"Note:" Dever says to the tape recorder in his breast pocket, "Sheriff

Jackson makes no move to disperse the crowd. He makes no move to quell public consumption of alcohol. Note to staff: research open container laws for state of Kentucky. Public intoxication laws, etc."

A white van with 'Eyewitness News 5 Alive!' emblazoned on the side, pulls into the parking lot like it carries bowls of goldfish. For a moment, the people in the lot are silent as the magnitude of the moment sinks in. This is going to be big. This is going to be on television. Then some bespectacled giant breaks the spell by raising his fist and loosening a sound from his mouth like a factory whistle. The gesture and cry are taken up by the crowd, joining them in a common destiny that spreads beyond the boundaries of the forests and offal-splotched pastures that surround them for miles in either direction. Whatever it is they are about to be a part of, it will be broadcast, it will be preserved. They are part of something bigger than themselves now, something so big that maybe they don't even understand their own importance, their own place in history. It's almost like being famous, which is next door to immortality. *Television.*

The van comes to rest next to the sheriff's cruisers and the crowd surges forward, forsaking that advance contingent of uniformed Sons who are passing out pamphlets and trying to get people to sign a clipboard. The side door of the van slides open and a man steps out. Onto his shoulder he hefts a camera the likes of which no one in the crowd has ever seen. The man sweeps the camera across the crowd and as he does people stop in their tracks as if their brains have just been erased by some magnetism shot from the lens. They touch their hair, straighten their posture, and stuff their shirttails into their pants. The cameraman unshoulders the camera and grins. Two other men emerge from the van, dragging gear, some of which they attach to their belts and some of which they wear on their backs. There is a pole with a fuzzy microphone on the end and a pole with a spotlight. The crowd watches the work of the men with something approaching reverence, giving them a respectful margin of room to carry out their technical rites.

Then Shawnee Dew steps from the van and there is the audible intake of breath. She is smaller than they thought she would be, and wearing more makeup than she should. Gobs of makeup. Way too much makeup. A face painted on a face really. But Shawnee Dew's face. And her clothes are smart and elegant just like they are at six and eleven, but she wears running shoes. And her legs aren't as long and slender as everyone imagined they would be, but nevertheless, they're attached to Shawnee Dew. Up there. Where her legs attach.

Another shout and another round of clenched fists for Shawnee Dew. Yeah! Then Shawnee stands before the camera in the glow of the spotlight and speaks. "Testing, testing, check, check." And those who are close enough hear that the voice she uses is Shawnee Dew's voice and this registers on their faces as they nod to one another. Yep. Shawnee Dew's voice. And the people behind her lean in around her shoulders in the hopes of getting in the picture, looking serious and grave, as though they are about momentous business. But a boy occasionally hops into view above their heads and a girl farther back rides someone's shoulders. Shawnee returns to the van and can be seen through the door reading a novel while the technicians continue their equipment checks, occasionally turning on the spotlight causing people to gather in the glow and scowl and look putout and threatening, like this light they sought is an invasion of their privacy.

"This is going to be a catastrophe," Dever says. "An unmitigated disaster."

102   FORTY-FIVE MINUTES after the Sons of Liberty vowed to breech the entrance of Howard Johnson's, the plate glass door still stands inviolate, giving our reflections back with the coming of dark. Dever, Shorty, and I stand guard while the Sheriff takes calls on his cell phone in my office, speaking in muffled tones but occasionally laughing out loud. Dever switches off the tape recorder in his pocket.

"You're finished mister," he whispers to me.

"Yeah," the short lawyer says. "When this is over you're out on your Jew ass."

The sheriff steps back into the lobby. "I'm happy to report that the Grand Master's motorcade is this minute approaching the outskirts of town and has only been held up because he is working the case of a white girl who was assaulted by a gang of Mexicans. He's been making calls and checking up on this and that to make sure her rights are protected and the Mexicans don't walk away scot-free like they usually do. Anyway, that's what his guys are telling folks out there."

"Note:" Dever says to his tape recorder. "Sheriff Jackson appears to be severely undermanned for the task at hand."

I ALWAYS THOUGHT it was a rule that you had to ride a Harley if you were in motorcycle gang, but when the Journeymen roar into the parking lot they are on Hondas and Suzukis and Yamahas and Triumphs and big boxy BMWs and other bikes that look like they were thrown together from spare parts lying around someone's yard. The bikes are old and none of them shines. But Brenda Gipson is hanging onto the back of one of them and she glitters. In cut off jeans and a tiny-t, that girl sparkles. I watch her climb off the motorcycle and extract a wedge of denim from the cleft of her crotch. Oh to be that piece of cloth, that sweet, sweat, sodden cotton. Then I lose her in the crowd.

Sheriff Jackson chuckles. "You know, it used to be real hard to get someone to even run for sheriff down here because it usually meant you'd have to shoot one of these boys. Then their kin would come after you. That's how I got to be sheriff. My predecessor went to serve papers and took both barrels standing on the front porch. I've never had real serious trouble with them though. They aren't so bad really. They just drink too much and follow their dicks around, but I find that's pretty much the average up and down the hollar."

"Sheriff," Dever says to his recorder. "I request that you take action to disperse the crowd immediately."

A pick-up truck with out-of-state plates pulls into the lot and the Buick that has been parked in the lot all day vacates its space and the pick-up pulls in. The truck has a sheet metal platform attached to the top of the cab with steps rising from the bed. There are mounts for speakers and mounts for microphones and mounts for flags and the Sons work with military precision until the vehicle is festooned with all these things.

"Here we go, here we go," the Sheriff says, nodding to the top of the service road where cars have pulled onto the berm. "Action in the bull pen!"

Silhouettes of figures in plumed hats move in front of headlights like characters in a shadow play, getting into order, installing thick flagpoles into the belts they wear. Then the headlights are killed, torches are lit, and here comes the Sons of Liberty.

The crowd, unable to restrain itself, runs up the hill to meet the procession like it's a liberating army. Flashbulbs snap. Reporters from local papers struggle to think of questions and walk backwards at the same time. The technicians from Eyewitness 5 form a protective wedge around

Shawnee Dew and position themselves on the service road. As the parade collides with the crew, the spotlight comes on, the wedge opens up, and Shawnee is inserted directly in front of the Grand Master, who slows his pace to accommodate her backpedaling. She asks a question into the microphone, the Grand Master answers it, looking confidently into the camera.

"Yeah! Yeah! *WhooOOOO!!*"

The Grand Master stops at the curb where hours earlier Dever and the short lawyer had disembarked from their cab. His honor guard continues its two-column onslaught, forming a torch lit walkway between the Grand Master and the door he has vowed to breech.

The Grand Master walks to the door, three flag bearers behind him. Though he is considerably shorter than the Sons who stand around him, the altitude of his plume exceeds theirs by several inches and as he draws nearer the cosmetic preparation of his face becomes shockingly apparent. The boundaries of his lips extend onto the skin of his face and a pencil has aided the definition of his eyebrows. Every bit as much as Shawnee Dew, the Grand Master is ready for his close up.

The sheriff steps out the door.

The Grand Master moves into the lawman's personal space with a pugnacious air. The Journeymen push aside other supporters and jostle the television crew. The cameraman tries to stand his ground and gets the camera shoved hard into his face.

"Hit the little twerp!" shouts the motorcyclist Brenda rode in with, a laughing youth with .01% embroidered on his denim vest. "Rip his throat out!" he shouts gleefully. "Kill the sonofabitch. Kill him! Kill him!"

The other Journeymen take up the cry hilariously. "Kill him, kill him, kill him!" they shout, punching the air like they're at a pep rally. The Grand Master smiles smugly at the sheriff, but the sheriff smiles back. One of the Sons behind the Grand Master lets out a rebel yell that seems a little hollow, a bit undermined by the knee-slapping, hold-the-stomach, mirth of these motorcyclists.

The Grand Master opens his mouth and something like southern kazoo music comes out.

"Waa wa-wa wo wa wowoo wat wa wats."

The sheriff leans forward. "Huh?"

On the inside of the door, I lean forward too.

"Wutter yew gwanna dew t' pertick mah rats!" the Grand Master says, but he is visibly thrown off his script. What kind of sheriff says huh? He still delivers the words but the spirit has fled.

The sheriff shakes his head and cants his ear. "What?"

"His *rats!*" .01% shouts. "Cain't you unnerstan English? Yew some kinda ferener er sumpon? Yew jes git off the boat? His rats, goddamnit! What're you gonna to do to protect his *rats?*"

Brenda falls over laughing. She's drunk and stoned and full of chewed up Oxycontin. That girl really knows how to party and seeing her like this makes me nostalgic. Makes me miss the times we had.

The Grand Master glances around.

"Kill 'em! Kill 'em! Kill 'em!" the Journeymen shout, pushing in on the color guard of the Sons of Liberty.

"The sheriff's got to do something!" Dever says. "Why isn't he doing anything?"

The Grand Master spins on his feet and walks back through the ranks of his guard, his hands clasped over his head like he's just won a victory. He mounts the bed of the truck, then mounts the stairs to the platform over the cab. He starts to speak, but a beer bottle flies end over end spewing foam like a whirly-gig firework, arching over the Grand Master's head and smashing on the asphalt behind him. For a moment, he must hope against hope the bottle was thrown as an expression of exuberant solidarity, like Palestinians firing guns at funerals. Sure the bullets come down with the velocity with which they go up, but the shooters don't *mean* to kill fellow mourners. Perhaps that's how the Grand Master tries to think of this bottle. Not as an assault, but as a rowdy show of support. He raises his fist in the air. "Whooooooooo!" he says.

"Whooooooooo!" the crowd answers. And from my spot behind the door I detect another thought is dawning on the Sons of Liberty who stand in the bed of the truck. There is a restlessness about them. One points. They see something I don't, some movement among this well-tanned, brown-eyed, dark haired motorcycle gang.

"Sheriff...?" the Grand Master says uncertainly into the microphone, beckoning him with his hand to come forward. Sheriff Jackson waves amiably. A barrage of ball bearings fill the air.

Noncombatants run to their cars, opening a more direct line of fire for the Journeymen who propel their missiles with slingshots.

"What? What?" Dever ejaculates the words.

The Grand Master goes down momentarily then appears again, surfing the upraised fists of the crowd, his face the picture of terror, then disappears again beneath the waves of the mob. The camera crew, sans Shawnee Dew, ventures too close to the maelstrom and is likewise pulled in, then spit back out, sans equipment.

"We've got to *do* something," Dever says, his eyes wild, crazed. "We've got to do *some*thing. We've got to take action."

"Then do something," I say.

"I will! You just watch!"

"Go ahead," I say. "Do it if you're man enough. Do it now."

"You just watch me!"

"I'm watching."

Dever rushes out the door and disappears into the sweating brown riot. I turn to the short lawyer. "What about you?" I say. "What are you going to do?"

He shoves the door open a bit, and lets it close again. Then, gathering his courage, bolts out as if bailing from an airplane. The access road is suddenly pulsing with the flashing lights of cruisers. Deputies wielding nightsticks pile out of a paddy wagon.

The Journeymen run to their motorcycles. "Let's roll! Let's roll! Fire 'em up!" Brenda and .01% bounce across the yard and down the drainage ditch and up the other side, dropping over the lip of the curb, turning west and roaring away on the highway, going, going, gone. They're all leaving. All the Journeymen. Carefully rolling through the yard and scattering in the night, some turning east, some turning west, leaving nothing but the broken glass of the Sons' vehicles. Windshield glass and headlight glass throbbing blood red in the flashing light like jagged rubies. The Grand Master is lead by, naked and weeping, his bloated belly and spindly legs crimson. His supporters follow, likewise bloodied, their hands secured with thin plastic bands. And in their midst, the short lawyer, one shoe off and one shoe on, and Dever, his breast pocket ripped from his coat. The Eyewitness 5 Alive cameraman stands baffled, speechless, looking down at the disemboweled pile of smashed circuitry that was his equipment. "You have the right to remain silent," Sheriff Jackson says through a bullhorn. Shawnee Dew peeks from the van, seeing if it's safe to come outside.

I light a cigarette.

The door stands before me unmolested and unthreatened, a symbol of nothing. One side you push, the other side you pull. Either way you stand pretty much in the same place.

I step outside.

The sky doesn't crush me. I don't fly off into space. But turning back I see a man encased in the door frame — boxed behind the glass like some sainted corpse, like Lenin, or Mao or Eva Peron — and his lips are moving, forming some word.

My keys are in my pocket. So is my credit card.

By the time I hit the parking lot, I break into a jog.

Pitbull

*Upon release a dog must immediately start across
the pit. He may push, pull or drag himself so long
as he does not stop, waver or hesitate.*
— Pit rule 12, the Cajun variation

MASSIEVILLE, KENTUCKY WAS cold when Hollister Gosney
rode through at four a.m. on the first day of winter of 1977. Too cold. The
kind of dry Arctic air that made snow pass into vapor with no intervening
liquid state. Cold that grew frozen waterfalls out of cliffs and blew through
layers of leather and denim like it wasn't even there. Crow killing cold. Tree
shattering cold.

Other than a few dilapidated red-brick antebellums huddled at the
crossroad, most of the housing in Massieville consisted of older mobile
homes, and the flood last March had hit them hard, knocking them off
their blocks, stripping away aluminum skirting, tearing at the pink insulation beneath the floor boards. During the deluge, some people had moved
in with kin in higher hollows. Others had camped in the National Forest
until the water receded. Then, when the carpeting had dried enough for the
stink to be stood, they dragged the trailers back to their lots, jacked them
up on blocks again and hammered together new outhouses from the tin
sheets and plywood that had once belonged to neighbors upstream. Now,
in December, most of Massieville was taking on winter in shelter better
suited for chicken coops. Hollister didn't know if they were tough or just
plain stupid.

He took the back way to Sim Keever's house, the long way through
the Gorge, winding over a Forest Service road bordered by stone on one
side and air on the other. The old shovelhead nearly choked on the steep

incline reaching up to Nada Tunnel, then gathered its mechanical breath and climbed into the black hole. How many times had Hollister been through this single lane passage? His school bus had gone through it every day, twice a day, for eleven years. How many was that? Thousands? Still he felt uneasy going through the mountain, suspecting it bore some resemblance to the state of death.

A shiver shook him, whether from the rock all around or from anticipation of what he was about to do, Hollister did not know. He did know certain standards of human conduct had to be enforced. Rules basic to society's function had to be maintained. An unraveling thread put the whole fabric at risk and if it fell to him to put things right, then he was the man for the job. That willingness to do one's duty regardless of what it might be was what it meant to be a man. And by God, a bet was a bet.

It had been at the Black Jackson Bar and Cultural Center back in August, when the air was full of humidity and the sweet smell of tobacco, that Sim had said the Gosney strain of Old Family Reds was played out, was vicious enough but too inbred to fight intelligently, and that his dog Spike could take Hollister's dog Ace easy.

Hollister laughed in his face. "I got five hundred dollars says Ace can kill Spike."

Sim said nothing for a moment, looking into his beer as though it contained something to see, suspecting perhaps that he had just gotten in over his head. "I'll take your bet," he'd said that day in August.

Hollister's headlight finally caught the icy fangs at the mouth of the long throat of the tunnel. It was cold. Way too cold to be on a motorcycle.

IN THE DISTANCE, a wave hit the sinking junk and seemed to swallow the little boat. Melvin King, second officer of the Australian freighter *Keira Ann*, turned away from the rail, cupped his be-ringed fingers against the wind and lit his next Dunhill off his last. The South China Sea was full of nasty things, things like sea snakes and hammerheads and great whites. Things that had no truck with human sensibility, with heartbreak, or loneliness, or foreknowledge of death. For the last few months, the South China Sea was also full of these boats.

Mel inhaled the cigarette like it contained the only air on the planet. He smoked too much, drank too much, ate too much, and felt bad about it all. But what else was there to do? The *Keira Ann* was a rust bucket repository of rejects, the kind of assignment a sailor draws when the directors want him to quit. Mel's own slide down the merchant marine food chain began when a certain "instability" was noted on a review. Management did nothing for awhile, waiting for him to get over it. When he didn't, they assigned him to the *Keira Ann*.

Mel flipped the half-smoked Dunhill end over end, watching it arc into the water. Death by drowning wasn't supposed to be such a bad way to go if you didn't fight it. That's what he'd heard anyway. He watched the sinking junk and considered the advantages of being a sea snake. No conscience. No memories. No music playing in the head. Just breed, eat and die.

But he wasn't a sea snake. Wearily, he climbed the ladder to the bridge.

"What are you doing, Mister King?" Captain Sorrel asked, football sized rings of sweat under each arm. Though the heat was stifling, the captain wore a tie and had his top button fastened.

Mel checked his watch. 16:13. "The boat off starboard. I'm entering it in the log. I guess you didn't see it, Captain. There's a sinking junk flying a distress flag."

Sorrell stared straight ahead. McGill, who was decorating the bridge with strands of plastic mistletoe, grunted a single tone chuckle. Mel continued the log entry.

"Mr. King, if we stop for every derelict junk we will never deliver a cargo of edible bananas to Vladivostok."

"Unfortunately, there's not a whole lot else we can do. International Law of the Sea and all," Mel said. "You're not suggesting we pass a sinking ship are you?"

"Very well, Mr. King. Very well then. Prepare a boarding party of two other men. They're all likely to be dead on board—they always are—so you are to personally go through each and every pocket and inventory the contents. Is that clear? I don't want this responsibility delegated. You are to personally go through *each* pocket and collect all identifying papers of the deceased."

McGill laughed again.

"Come on," Mel said, spotting the sailor. "You and Rosen are on the boarding party."

Approaching from downwind in an inflatable Zodiac, the stench of human rot was overwhelming. Rosen jacked a round of double-00 buckshot into the chamber of the stainless steel Remington. Mel pushed the trigger of his bullhorn and hailed the boat, first in English, then in Vietnamese. No response. The boat was riding low and would sink in a couple of hours, five at most.

Mel leaned toward the rail of the junk but couldn't make the step. McGill goosed the motor and Mel hurtled forward, catching the rail at belt level so that his legs hung overboard while his hands grasped at what at first seemed to be a pile of rags. Mel lurched from the corpse convulsively, hitting the deck hard with his shoulder. The roll of the junk slid the body toward him and Mel scuttled backward like a crab. He wasn't touched by the dead man, but the water washed over him and seemed to permeate his nose and mouth with the taste of corruption.

The corpse, swollen so that the button of his pants had popped, was entangled in rigging. He had a half-inch hole in the right side of his forehead where a bullet had entered and a chunk the size of a sand dollar had blown out behind the left ear where the round had exited. Another body, shot twice through the chest, was wedged under the port rail, flesh split with bloat.

Mel took out a handkerchief and tied it around his face. He didn't know why people did that, because it did nothing to diminish the smell, but still he felt better wearing the cloth. Maybe it had something to do with hiding, with going in disguise in the presence of an obviously hovering reaper. He squatted at the open hatch and peered below deck. A plastic cup floated by with a figure printed on it, a blonde child with impossibly large blue eyes and pouting red lips. "Precious Moments," the cup read. A sandal made from the tread of a worn tire bobbed nearby. Then the almond shape of Asian eyes slid into view, unfocused, unseeing, black hair splaying out in the oil splotched water. The boat was a shark magnet if ever there was one.

In the stern, under a windbreak made of bamboo and tattered olive drab canvas, lay a stack of reed mattresses, and on the mattresses, a young woman and a child. The boy was naked and lay face down on the woman's torso, bowels voided in death but the tissue yet unswollen. The woman's face, unusually angular for a Vietnamese, was blistered around the lips and nose. The eyes were matted shut and her T-shirt was pulled up as if to give the child, a boy, access to her breasts. On a chain around her neck was a locket. These two had died only recently. With the toe of his boot, Mel nudged the boy's limp body aside.

The woman's eyes slammed open and her hand rose holding 39 ounces of dripping American steel. It was but a twitch of her thumb that brought the .45 to bear.

Years later Mel claimed his whole life passed before his eyes, that in that moment of terror he grasped the irony of a man surviving two tours of duty in the Iron Triangle only to become a casualty years after the war was over. But really he thought nothing. He saw the skin under the nail of her index finger grow a whiter shade and thought nothing. She pulled the trigger; the hammer fell; again nothing.

Her left hand shot up and jacked back the slide expelling the sodden bullet. Mel slapped the gun up over her head as the slide clanked forward, loading another round into the chamber. He went down on top of her. Two shots fired, then the slide locked open, empty. Thrashing, trying to find his groin with her knees, she caught his cheek in her teeth.

Mel jumped off, holding the wound and the woman spat out the skin and was up, kicking at his knees, driving him back from her dead child. Rosen came aboard and got an elbow in the nose for his trouble. Countering with a roundhouse, he sent her sprawling to the deck where she continued kicking up at them.

"Stand back!" McGill called from the skiff, leveling the shotgun. "I'll get her."

"Put it down!" Mel said. "Cut the line and come aboard. That's an order, McGill." But the sailor kept the butt of the gun against his cheek. "If you shoot her you'd better shoot me too because I swear to God I'll kill you. Bring a piece of line and come aboard. Now."

Mel could feel the binocular gaze of the *Keira Ann* as they held the woman down and bound her hand and foot.

"Skiff's gone," McGill said when they had her tied. "We used the line to tie up some stinkin' gook and the skiff floated away. Now here we stand on a sinking junk and the skiff's gone."

"Shut up, McGill."

The Zodiac had drifted maybe fifteen feet.

It's best not to think about it. It's best to just do it and get it over with. Mel stripped to briefs and dove into the South China Sea.

The worst was the initial encapsulation in the blurry green when the mind entertained a fraction of fear that the battle between buoyancy and gravity would shift and one would sink like lead. Then, just as suddenly, he was up out of the dark, still largely blind, gasping. Mel swam to the skiff and tried to pull himself in. Lacking the strength, he pushed the skiff back. The junk gave a pop and a groan. McGill and Rosen stood at the rail, the woman between them, still struggling, still looking back to where the child lay.

There was nothing gentle about the way they threw her into the bottom of the skiff. Rosen tried to help Mel in but the woman bent at the waist and thrust her bound feet causing the inflatable to rear up. Mel let go of the gunwale and slipped again into the watery netherworld, emerging a second later to a sound like someone tenderizing veal. He managed to roll aboard under his own strength.

"Enough," he gasped.

McGill continued pummeling the woman though she was already unconscious.

Mel found the shotgun and put the barrel against McGill's back. "I said enough. Just get on the motor and get us away."

Mel cradled the woman's head. An eyetooth hung by a thread and her nose was broken but she still breathed. He pulled her nose out from her face, then pushed it back where it belonged. He stuck the tooth in its socket. A pain started in his chest and migrated out his left arm.

"Permission to ask a question, sir," McGill said over the outboard. A drop of water tinged with Dorian Grey fell from Mel's hair to the woman's forehead. He looked up at McGill. Every vein in the sailor's face stood clear. "Just who do you suppose shot all those people back there?"

THE PITBULL WAS made by centuries of cruel men — first in the British Isles, then throughout the Anglo world — men who bred not for color or conformation or even strength, but for a shadow trait, something that couldn't be seen, or weighed, or found in an autopsy. It was called gameness and it was that thing that made the dog unrelenting. To isolate such a characteristic was to banish sentimentality, for if a dog once curred — that is to turn from the face of fight — he was a pollutant to the race and a thing to be despised. He was a coward, and was allowed to be torn apart in the pit. So it came to pass after many generations that there was not a creature in the world close to the pitbull, not in pure blind viciousness, nor in trueness of heart.

113

Hollister emerged from the tunnel into air laden with wood smoke and livestock. He pushed the gear lever into neutral and cut the motor. People lived on this side of the mountain and none of them needed to hear his punched pipes going by. He would coast the rest of the way.

Sim Keever lacked character and Hollister had suspected he would cheat if he could, so when it was time for Hollister to wash Sim's dog, he'd taken extra care to spread the hair on the top of Spike's neck, looking for red pepper. He smelled the dog. He touched his tongue to the animal's skin, then lifted him into the tub of warm water and scrubbed him down good. Spike was lean and muscled from running on a mill, and his neck and jaws were hard from hanging from a deer hide hoisted in a tree. Hollister lifted the dog from the water, dried him, wrapped him in a blanket and carried him to the appropriate corner under the ever-watchful eye of Sim's corner man. Sim, accompanied by Buck Jackson, Hollister's man, brought Ace in and washed him in the same water. The two dogs crouched low and would not break eye contact.

"Corner men, out of the pit," the referee called when Ace was dry. "Handlers to your corners."

The pit was sixteen feet each way, with two scratch lines chalked on the canvas floor twelve and one-half feet apart. Hollister tried to stare Sim down as the referee recited the rules because Hollister knew there was nothing in the dog that wasn't in the man, and if fear was in the man he would pass it to the dog and the dog would cur, which was to lose. Sim put on a brave face but showed a little slippage around the eyes.

"Face your dogs," ordered the ref.

Hollister positioned Ace's head and shoulders showing fair from between his knees, his hands at Ace's chest.

"Let go!"

The dogs had run to each other on that day while men shouted in guttural tones that weren't words. The timekeeper had checked his watch and noted the time on a pad under the date August 16. That was how it had started.

Shivering, Hollister rolled silently into Sim's frozen driveway.

THE CREW OF the *Keira Ann* gathered to gawk as if the woman were a mermaid plucked from the distant depths.

"What's she saying?"

"I don't know," Mel said.

"I thought you spoke that lingo."

"I thought I did too."

She said it again, barely audible. The exact same thing. Five or six syllables.

"It doesn't even sound like Vietnamese," Mel said.

"Let's give 'er a bath."

"Get back to work," Mel said. "Everyone."

The men filed out like children sent to bed. Mel raised her upper lip and inspected the tooth, snug in the gum. He knelt and sighted along the silhouette of her nose. The bridge was too prominent for Vietnamese. She was Eurasian, of partial French parentage probably. The Frogs had left thousands of half-breeds in the wake of their own Indo-China catastrophe and — while the Americans and Australian fools rushing in found these mixed race girls to be beautiful beyond compare — the Vietnamese treated them as outcasts.

Mel opened the locket. A girl, not much more than a child, sat on the knee of an American. Behind them, the stacked sandbags of firebase fortification. She was wearing an oversized shirt bearing the screaming eagle insignia of the 101st Division. The American was bare-chested, dark, and well put together at the shoulders and neck. At first glance it was almost believable that she was one of those kids who followed GIs around begging for chewing gum. But the drape of her fingers over his collarbone and the pressure of his hand upon her thigh gave the lie to the notion that this was a relationship based on Juicyfruit. Mel's own Emily was about the age of the girl on the American's lap and, though he hadn't seen her in almost a year, he hoped she never talked to boys with eyes so brutally blue.

He shut the locket and laid it gently against the girl's skin.

She spoke again, shaking her head as if to clear the fog. What was it? Six syllables repeated like a mantra. He stroked her cheek with his finger. How long had it been since he had touched a woman? Something like a memory came back and told him all he had come to lack.

Turning on the hot water in the sink, he remembered a practical nurse bathing his dying mother. He had turned away then. Now he wished he had paid attention. He tested the water against his wrist and dampened the wash cloth. He would start by cleaning the rope burns on her hands and feet. There was Mercurochrome somewhere. She muttered in her unknown tongue again, moving her arms, trying to hold the air, finding nothing in her grasp.

Melvin King worked quietly, combining strength and gentleness, until all her wounds were clean and she lay on fresh sheets. He held her hand for several minutes. "I know who you are," he whispered. "You're the angel sent to catch a man as he falls."

McGill came through the door. "What'd you say? Are you talking to her?" He carried something Mel at first thought was a folded raincoat. "After the pounding I gave her, I'm surprised she's not already dead." He unfolded the body bag and dropped it on the floor parallel to the bed. The inside of the bag was treated with white powder. "You didn't see how I got up under her ribs. You were under water," he smiled. "I tore her up inside."

"Get out, McGill."

"The captain wants you. I'm supposed to stay here and you're supposed to go."

"So you can put the pillow over her face? Get out before I kill you."

"The captain said … hey hands off!"

"Then get out!" Mel shoved the sailor.

"Oh you'll pay for that. I'll see you pay for that."

Mel finally got an IV dripping into a vein. Locking the infirmary door behind him, he went to his cabin, turned on some of his favorite music, put on his white lamé jumpsuit and took a teddy bear from his trunk. It was a little lopsided, but he fluffed it some and it took on a more presentable shape.

He had bought the bear for Emily the last time he saw her. They had stayed at his aunt's house in Wooroloo because he wanted the two to get to know each other and because he wanted his daughter to see where he was raised. Here were the two females who bounded his life and the only issue they could agree on was that Mel had indeed been tugged in a strange direction. Otherwise, Aunt Edna didn't care for Sydney figures of speech and Emily claimed nausea at the very smell of the older woman's cooking. Nor did the quaintness of Wooroloo hold any charm for the girl. On their last night together he let her choose a movie and then drove forty silent miles to the theater, stopping to eat at a café where she made it obvious she was embarrassed to be with him. During the movie — starring a strangely effeminate leading man whose range did not get much beyond a smirking leer — it was Mel's turn to be embarrassed. Emily had laughed loud at the witless double entendres to let him know she understood the smutty gags.

On the way to the train station the next morning, she finally spoke. "I wonder what Mom and Dad did this weekend."

Before she boarded, he tried to embrace her but it came off as an uneasy dance that ended in kissing the air close to her cheek.

"Why do you want to look like that, Melvin?" Aunt Edna had said as soon as he returned to the house. "You're not a teenager anymore." He walked by letting the comment pass. He just wanted to get back to the sea. "I guess Emily didn't like the music you bought her," Edna called after him.

In the spare bedroom, on the floor, was the cassette tape of *Viva Las Vegas* and the teddy bear. He left the tape where it was, perhaps because he already had two copies or maybe because it represented a degree of rejection he didn't want to acknowledge. But when he packed up he took the bear with him and every time he ran across it he wondered why. Now he knew. The haywire lines of his life were finally converging. He fluffed the bear and looked at its face, at its button eyes and little round tongue. The cassette tape sang.

117

> I don't know why you'd run,
> What you're running to or from,
> All I know is I've got to bring
> You ho-ome.

Mel rewound the tape and listened to the song again. "I'll be damned," he said.

SIM KEEVER HAD gotten a job working third shift at the sawmill. Because his wife was dead, his children stayed with grandparents at night, a couple hundred yards down the switchback road or about fifty yards as the sparrow flies, for the land was very steep.

Spike picked up the presence of a stranger on the wooden steps and barked.

"Good boy. Good Spike," the voice on the other side of the door said. "Spike, sit. Sit, Spike." The dog quit barking. "Good boy. Good Spike."

Hollister Gosney kicked the door in.

"Good boy. Come. You smell my dogs don't ya boy. Yeah. Good boy.

Sit."

Hollister opened the refrigerator and found a pack of baloney. The meat hit the floor like a Hollywood slap. He dumped what was left of a carton of eggs. A half-full jar of mayonnaise shattered. Spike cocked his head quizzically.

"Last meal, boy. Come an' get it."

Hollister popped the top of a Strohs and went looking for the thermostat, he was so cold, so chilled to the bone. He plugged in the Christmas tree and sat in Sim's old recliner. An exhausted pack of Kools and a disposable lighter were on the endtable beside a thick, short, kindergarten-made candle with glitter embedded in the wax. It figured. A lowlife bastard like Keever *would* smoke menthols. Hollister lit one of his Camels, then the candle. The tree was a cedar, and though it wasn't a proper Christmas tree, it filled the trailer with a comfortable scent. There weren't many presents and they were all wrapped in the same blue paper printed with the worshipful Wise Men offering their gifts to a glowing baby Jesus. It was so obvious this radioactive infant was the Messiah that even the stupid sheep had that knowing look in their eyes. Crowning the scrawny evergreen, atop the spiraling string of stale popcorn, the angel, arms outstretched, presided over the meager largesse. She was blonde. Always blonde. Why not brunette? Brunettes were nice. Hell, why not a red head?

Hollister flicked ashes into Sim's ashtray, a heavy steel affair, square with an equilateral triangle and the word ARMCO stamped into the dish. He hurled the tray at the Sony's screen, which deflected the missile without sustaining so much as a crack.

"I'll be damned," he said to Spike, who looked up from his feast. Hollister went to the kitchen and drained another Strohs while standing in the light of the refrigerator. He picked up a metal-framed dinette chair patched with duct tape and charged the television, embedding the legs of the chair deep in the single eye. There. It looked like modern art, like something some idiot from New York would pay a million dollars for.

Spike looked up, wagging his tail, egg whites dripping from his muzzle. Hollister rubbed the nub of Spike's torn ear. He was a good dog — a better dog than Sim was a man — and it was a shame he had to die. Hollister flipped open his easy-out blade. It's best not to think about it. It's best to just get it over with. But he would drink another beer first.

The two dogs had climbed each other on the day of the fight, facing on hind legs, each trying to push the other down. Spike got his teeth into Ace's neck, but it was only in the loose flesh and Ace turned inside his skin and took Spike by the ear, ripping it where it joined the head. "That's a turn!" the referee shouted, pointing to Sim but looking to the timekeeper. "Pick up free of holds."

Sim and Hollister ran to their dogs and tried to pull them apart but Ace had seized the opportunity of Spike's turn to grasp the dog's leg. Ace knew what he had and sought neither to rip nor tear but to crush, and he was loath to give up such an advantage just because his master was telling him to.

"I'm breaking the lock!" the ref shouted to the timekeeper, who duly noted the call. The referee inserted the tip of a ram's horn between Ace's jaws and pried them apart. Sim and Hollister carried their dogs back to their scratch lines. Having turned, it was Spike, shaking his head and slinging blood, who had to scratch, who had to attack across the pit. Ace had inflicted a good wound, bleeding freely, and it would stand in his favor.

"Let go!" the ref called, and Spike charged across the pit, his hind legs a little out of synch with his front. The dogs had exploded into each other that day, rolling across the pit, one on top, then the other, painting the canvas with blood and saliva.

Hollister sat in Sim's Lazyboy and watched the smoke of his cigarette level out between the ceiling and floor. Spike nuzzled his hand and sat expectantly in the hope that more food could be dumped on the floor. The dog bled and Hollister looked in his mouth and saw that it was but a nick on the tongue from the broken jar. It didn't matter anyway. Hollister felt Spike's neck, thick like the barrel of an artillery piece.

"Come, boy." The dog moved closer, wagging his tail. "Sit."

Hollister opened his knife again. He wondered about killing and the human desire for it. He had first killed a man when he was a teenager. Actually, he had killed another teenager, a kid who probably didn't weigh a hundred pounds soaking wet and carried a bolt-action rifle left over from the Second World War. Hollister had knelt by the boy. He had thought killing someone would make him different, would make him more of a man like he thought having sex would. But it hadn't made him different at all. Still he remembered both the dead boy and the crying girl like he had been with them yesterday and wondered if he didn't bear these memories exact because they were set to come back to him at some later time.

"Gonna take a trophy?" some guy from Arkansas had asked.

Hollister had looked at the dead boy and saw that he had been crying and thought about the girl and how she had cried too and how he had pushed her black hair back with his fingers and noticed the gentle swirls of her ear and said everything was going to be all right, it's going to be all right, it's going to be all right. "No," he had answered the Arkansan. "It would just be one more thing to carry."

Hollister got up from the Lazyboy for another beer, throwing out the butt end of a loaf of Velveeta for Spike.

The two dogs had fought for more than an hour that day in August, the wound on the side of Spike's head welling until blood pooled in some spots on the floor. Hollister had tried to estimate the amount. One pint. Two. How much blood did a dog have in him anyway? One dog would get a turn called, then the other, never out of curring but just out of the dynamics of fighting. On one such turn, Spike fanged Ace deeply in the flank.

"Take up your dogs in their holds," the referee called, indicating that Hollister and Sim should hold the animals close until they were unfanged. But Sim had pulled Spike away, making the puncture into a tear.

The crowd grew quiet and Sim's face was ashen.

"You dumb motherfucker," Hollister said.

"By the book I can only call it a foul," the ref said to Hollister. "You want to forfeit?"

"Why the hell should I forfeit? The sonofabitch already killed my dog. We'll just have to win."

Sim, his shirt soaked with blood, seemed not to hear when the ref called the first time. When he finally released Spike, the dog staggered, suddenly feeling the hit of massive hemorrhage.

"Let him come to us, boy. Let him come to us," Hollister said, holding Ace until Spike attacked. "I'm right here," Hollister said, positioning himself behind his dog. "Don't let him get me."

Ace met the onslaught head on, giving no ground, and even advancing some. Then a turn was called on Ace. It was a fair turn and a good call, but now Hollister's dog would have to cross the canvas to attack, and his entrails were already touching the floor.

"Let's call it a draw," Sim had said. "We can still save our dogs."

"We can't call it a draw because it ain't a draw," Hollister had answered.

In the cabinet over Sim's stove, Hollister found a half bottle of booze and a can of Vienna sausage. The whiskey was strong and went down in stages of oak smoke, candied cherries and fire. Spike ate the meat in a single gulp.

"Let's see what Daddy bought Becky for Christmas," Hollister said, turning to the tree and slicing open a present with his knife.

THE WOMAN DID not hold the stuffed bear as Mel hoped she would. Maybe she was not fooled by it. Maybe she was just too weak and hurt. He mixed honey and applesauce in a bowl, propped her up on pillows and tried to spoon a bit past her swollen lips.

"Help me out, Angel. One step in the right direction and we can go the distance. I know we can. You've come this far. Don't give up now."

Mel dabbed the food off her lips with a napkin. Her breathing was shallow and when he went to take her pulse he could not find it at first. His glance fell to the body bag. "We'll have none of this," he said, opening the porthole and throwing the bag into the sea. He maximized the drip of the IV.

"Mr. King?" Captain Sorrell tried the door. "You're ten minutes late for your shift."

"Go to hell."

There was silence from the other side of the door for a moment.

"Then it is true what they say about you. You *are* insane."

"Thank you," Mel said. "Thank you very much."

SIM'S PRESENT TO Becky was a porcelain baby in a gingham dress. Johnny was getting a model kit of a '57 Chevy and the kids had put a photograph in a gilded frame and wrapped it up for Daddy. The photo showed all four of them standing on the steps on a sunny day, a scrawny redbud straining to bloom to the side, Mommy and Becky in Easter hats. Though Mommy was thin and haggard and wore a cheap wig, she smiled. Sim wore a lime green leisure suit with the wide collars of his florid shirt hanging out over the jacket. John, chubby and squinting, wore a clip-on tie and white shirt that was too small.

Hollister drained the bourbon from the bottle.

"Hold!" Sim had cried that day in August when Ace drove Spike to

121

the canvas. "Enough!"

Hollister ran into the pit and laid Ace over. There was only one puncture on the intestine. He would patch it with paper towel and super glue. He would wash the dog's insides off and carefully reinstall them. He would sew the dog up with six pound fishing line, leaving a slot for drainage, and feed him antibiotics. Hollister stroked Ace's huge head. The story would spread about a dog so game. If Ace lived he would spend the rest of his life in stud service and make Hollister thousands of dollars.

"Pick up my cash, will you?" Hollister said to Buck Jackson. But Buck looked as if Sheriff Stone had just walked in with the Reverend Hutchinson.

"I can't let you take my money, Hollister," Sim said. "I need that money for my kids."

Hollister looked up into the barrel of the pistol, a .22 or .25. "Then you shouldn't've put it on a dog fight."

"I just need my money."

"You don't understand, you dumb sonofabitch. It ain't your money now," Hollister had said on that hot day. "And if you think this is over just because you got a gun in my face, you're wrong. Dead wrong."

Hollister crushed the framed photograph under the heel of his boot. Then the doll's head, then the model car. He flipped open his blade and spun unsteadily on Spike, but found himself caught in a strange pirouette that ended in a stab at the Christmas tree, loosening a sound so plaintive that he wondered where it came from. The tree fell against the end table, against the lit candle, and began to burn at a small branch, shriveling the silver tinsel, then melting the insulation of the Christmas lights which shorted out the electricity, plunging the room into darkness illuminated only by the growing fire. The arm of Sim's chair slowly seared, then the curtains went up in a flash of heat and light. Black smoke curling at the ceiling took on an internal glow. Flashover. The trailer was about to explode.

Hollister ran out the door, falling on the steps where the dead woman had stood to be photographed. He staggered into the yard and turned to look at the flames lewdly licking at the door. He called out, but his voice was lost in the flames. The dog was still sitting by Sim's chair when Hollister took him by his collar and dragged him into the yard.

MEL TRIED TO shut down the doubt in his mind

Oh God (if there is a God),

grant me this prayer (if I have a prayer)

for the redemption of my soul (if I have a soul).

When the woman stopped breathing at sunset he put his hand on her chest and his mouth over hers.

HOLLISTER GOSNEY ROLLED back on the throttle and let Jim Beam take the curves.

Thundering up through the gears — third, fourth — roaring down the mountain. Wake up! Lay in your beds and cuss but know that Hollister Gosney is passing through and years from now you'll talk about it. You'll tell your grandchildren when you pass by the spot on the road that you remember hearing Hollister ride by and how he was a gambler and a dogfighter and how he broke into a man's house and got all liquored up and burned the place down then flew off the side of the hill straight into hell. Fifth gear. Tears blowing back. Eighty-five. Ninety. Wake up dammit! Something is about to happen in your nothing life. That crazy sonofabitch Hollister Gosney is passing through like a fucking comet and you don't want to miss it.

Ninety-five.

One-hundred.

Hollister hung his feet back over the passenger pegs and lay his chest down on the gas tank, red hot fluid exploding in the heart, screaming a curse at the coming of dawn, but keeping a promise at the crest of the hill. Airborne.

MELVIN KING LET the atlas of North America fall from his lap. He leaned over the woman, opened the locket and looked at the two in the photograph one more time, the girl and her young warrior. The clouds behind them were dark and ready to burst, but the two looked so happy. They sat in a muddy jungle in the middle of a bloody war and they were happy. The American was glad to have this beautiful little half-breed on his lap and she was overjoyed to be there. In that way, Mel thought, it was perhaps a perfect day.

She reached up, and Mel hoped it was to take his hand, but it was only to take the locket. "Massieville," he heard her say. "Massieville, Kentucky."

Cult of the Side Wound

The screen of my laptop seems to float like a ghost in the darkness of my room at the Hotel Seville, the digital clock in the lower corner playing metronome to my insomnia.

3:13.

It drifts up and drifts down, one second fading in the time display as the next appears.

3:14.

It shrinks and hovers in my face, then grows and backs off in equal measure.

3:15.

Elevators rumble up the spine of the building, disgorging drunken Germans, guttural chatter fading as they stagger to their doors. Pipes wheeze bringing water up. Toilets cough sending it down.

3:16.

It's been twenty-seven and one half days. 660 hours. Almost 40,000 minutes. Nearly two and a half million seconds since I was with April at the Massieville Furnace Ruin.

No, that's wrong. I'm not counting the time zones between Kentucky and Spain. I click on a minimized screen, bringing up the image I downloaded yesterday at the Biblioteca Columbina. **heres a pic of me the guy who took it sad it wuz his fav wat do u think?** Then the hyper-linked words **contact me.**

The screen illuminates the leaves of printed articles scattered on my bed, giving them the tint of April's brown skin. *Temporal Lope Epilepsy and Hypergraphia*, the margins and backs of pages filled with my handwriting, a symptom of the very disease annotated. *Henry Darger: Realm of the Unreal,* similarly scribbled. *Open Letter to a Pedophile,* underlined and asterisked, arrows pointing to circled paragraphs. "The obsession pokes, kicks, jabs and punches at you every second of every day. You trust no one. Self-hate drenches you. You become secretive of everything."

Yet I feel the need to tell it, to nail down with words that which seems to have no words. I try again to explain, holding back nothing this time, typing fingers trying to touch each tactile subtlety, each nuance of taste and smell, and the details lead once more to the imagery of those darkest of Internet domains. But that's not what it was like. Though those places are a representation, that's not the way it was at all. We discovered this thing unexpectedly. Innocently. Those jaded denizens of the cyber netherworld are counterfeits in comparison, poor players who strut their phony passion and try to cover their emptiness with studded leather and body piercing. I reread what I wrote and delete it, backspacing a letter at a time, unwilling to paint my magic child with the pigments of pornography.

It is not a confession I long to write. It is a suicide note.

Your honor, Laptop testifies, *I, who so well know the nature of Reed McCampbell's soul, do not suppose he feels one ounce of regret. If he could do it again, he would. There are no words in the vast hoard of my spell-checker to tell the entirety of his desire, the depth of his depravity. Deletion is the only cure for Reed McCampbell. Deletion.*

I play with words awhile — attempting a poem of all things — letting language run like water over that elfin body, letting it pool in fragrant hollows and conform to every angle and slope, searching out the most personal intimacies before running on, enriched. But it keeps coming out a syllable long or a syllable shy, so I save what I have and shut down the computer. Of course, I'll have to delete everything.

Delete? No, dear Laptop. My end necessitates yours too. I will smash your indelible memory to bits before I go.

THE STREETS OF Seville are deserted, last night's revelers having gone to bed and the morning workforce not yet about. But a baker is on the job and the smell of rising yeast mingles with the scent of the Rio Guadalquivir's own mixed bouquet of bloom and decay, flowing down from Cordoba to the Gulf of Cadiz.

The Cathedral's massive walls — still radiating yesterday's intense heat — have been recently washed in preparation for the celebratory mass of Cardinal Estevez' ninetieth birthday. And in the labyrinthine bowels of the Cathedral, the Biblioteca Columbina, with its bombproof, climate-controlled vaults, allegedly containing secret manuscripts in Columbus' own hand.

The Sisters of the Side Wound are still camped on the steps of the Door of Pardons in their filthy robes, their faces black as obsidian, their alms bowls containing water now. Most of them lay fitfully sleeping on blankets around the litter of their dying priest, or shaman, or whatever he is. Two Sisters breast-feeding their babies nod, recognizing me as a Cathedral regular now. When the Cathedral opens for early mass, the Sisters will split forces, one squad going from Cathedral door to Cathedral door, following the shade, begging. The others will bear the litter of their leader through the Door of Pardons into the Patio de los Naranjos so he can have his fingers in the water when an angel touches the Fountain of the Well. They sold what they had in Haiti and came to Seville months ago because the shaman had a vision. Now they lay on the steps of the Cathedral on the eve of the Cardinal's visit, an embarrassment no one knows how to address. It's rumored the Sisters call the saints by different names and worship Mary as God.

Wandering through already stifling streets, I light a Ducados, a habit I've reacquired in Spain, where everyone smokes, everywhere, all the time. Middle-aged men in silk suits, breathing deep in hotel lobbies, enjoying the warmth and weight in their lungs. Dark women dangling ashes over glasses of red wine in cafés, drowsy from the mild narcotic effect. Teenagers doing James Dean in ancient doorways, brooding over the nebulous curling. Spain is far too full of tragedy, too full of history circling in on itself, not to smoke.

Coming out on the Passeo Cristobal Colon, I make for Isabel's Bridge. The Guadalquivir is swift and there is a breeze blowing out of the east that can't be had in the city. Slipping the laptop off my shoulder, I light a Ducados and watch the current swirl. I light a Ducados off the last Ducados, then light another from that. Five smokes left. Four minutes each. Twenty minutes. I lean forward until my feet are off the sidewalk, holding the rail like a gymnast on parallel bars. The first tint of sun smears the sky behind the Giralda, the twelfth-century minaret incorporated into the Cathedral. That special subset of suicides called jumpers often travel thousands of miles to get to the right platform, the

Golden Gate Bridge perhaps, or the observation deck of the Empire State Building. April was three when I met her.

MY FIRST MEMORY of April Jackson has taken on the hue of another species of light, as though the translucence of spring leaves lent the time a separate reality, as though the cottonwoods dappling the Red River gave the Appalachian air more than the white fleece that drifted on the breeze and blew across the meadow, where twelve undergrad archaeology students waited to be told what to do next.

She came running down a Forest Service access trail in white cotton underpants, a turkey feather and wild flowers stuck in her mane. She ignored us, weaving around trenches and stacks of flat rocks that had allegedly been dragged up from the Red by a people who were smelting iron in Kentucky before the Mayflower landed. Three shorthaired dogs with heads like shovels ran circles around her, their ears cut clean to the skull, their rat tails wagging in subservient ecstasy. American pit bull terriers. She ran to a man who picked her up and threw her in the air.

Tall and broad with a Pall Mall stuck in his mouth, April's father was dressed only in cut-off painter's pants and work boots. A triangular patch of transplanted skin was on his forehead, an iron colored braid hung down his back, and he was covered with tattoos. An eagle's head was over his heart with a scroll in its beak, and his arms were etched with the jailhouse rendering of a snake, the forked tongue of which flicked at the nail of the middle finger of his right hand, then coiled thickly around forearm and bicep, draping his shoulder before disappearing in the undergrowth of neck beard only to reappear slithering down over the other shoulder and arm to the left hand, where the tail narrowed to a rapier point extending to the nail of his index finger: Duval Jackson.

Dr. Abbott was there too, trying to show a blueprint to Duval, who was more interested in making April shriek by blowing on her belly. Father and daughter were tanned the same dark shade and their irises contained the same glacial cast of blue, which seemed to suggest they may not have been born to the trappings of savagery after all, but rather embraced them by choice. Duval tried to hold the girl but she squirmed free, entangled her fists in the hair of his beard and the hair of his head and climbed him like a rock, pulling herself onto his shoulders and clamping her brown legs around his neck. Upon the achievement of this summit, the two finally deigned to look at us students, April with a degree of arrogance remarkable for one so young, Duval with the practiced glance of a man confident in his prejudices. He passed the same quick judgment on race horses and pit dogs and it had made him money.

An Asian woman shouted from the door of the farmhouse in a language I didn't understand. April answered in kind with nine or ten defiant syllables, bringing a stern retort from the door.

"Tell Mommy no!" she demanded of Duval, pulling his face into hers by the hair of his beard.

I was stunned. I thought I knew everything there was to know about this crypto-indigenous clan, yet I had no idea this little one, this little half-breed of a half-breed, existed — though I knew immediately what she was to me.

THERE HAS BEEN trouble in the South Transept of the Cathedral and men in white biohazard suits block the entrance. "Blood," a man next to me says, and the unexpected English word causes me to jump. "Someone placed blood on the tomb of Columbo." He leans forward and whispers. "They believe it is the Voodoos and they fear it is *human.*"

I walk down the block and enter the cathedral through the Puerta De La Asuncion. The Sisters of the Side Wound stand on the steps, bowls in hand. I drop a bill and get an incantation.

The church is cool and cavernous, full of quiet echoes and the smell of votive candles. An army of nuns with dust cloths reams the smallest ornate crevices. A man in a Komatsu cherry picker runs a vacuum hose over the upper reaches of the vaults of the Capilla Mayor. Another buffs the tiles of a closed section of floor before the Capilla de la Virgin de la Antigua, the statue of the virgin called the Ancient One. Cardinal Estevez is coming and a good impression must be made.

I descend the steps to the Biblioteca and the scowling librarian-priest asks to see my card, as he does every morning. I sit in the same glass cubicle I sit in everyday, plug in my laptop and log on to the library's server. Glowering, the priest retreats to his own cubicle to monitor my suspicious wanderings, compiling evidence, I suspect, to revoke my membership. I check in on *The Darger Project,* peruse a few of Darger's paintings of the Vivian Girls then read a little from the latest transcription of the 15,000 page novel discovered after his death. Darger is great grist for the priest I figure. Besides being insane, hypergraphic and pedophilic, the artist was a devout Catholic and his obsessively detailed scenes of vivisected little girls only retells the stories of the saints, which is full of mutilated virgins.

I check in on April's web site and there she is. Or least the picture I took of her. Perched on my swivel chair in gym shorts, knees propped under chin, heels of bare feet on the edge of the seat, toes of the right foot bent down, toes of the left foot point up exposing the creamy underside of the digits, blending to Reubenesque russet on the ball of the foot. But it is her face that draws the eye. The moment before taking the picture I'd said something I shouldn't and she has the look of a little girl lost, that look that makes a man yearn to protect and exploit simultaneously.

The site has had sixty-six hits since it went up yesterday.

god April your really cute!!!! writes jburk66@yahoo. you plan to post most pictures????

i want the picture all nite and now i want to whisper want i want to do, adds 00369@ser01 I I.

129

April,
Allow me to introduce myself. My name is Dawson Moloch and I am a Hollywood agent. I would like to know more about you and see more of your photos. I believe you may be part of the small percent of the world's women for whom life can hold untold riches and pleasure- if you have the courage to make it happen. In particular, who took this astonishing photograph?

p.s. you're not a cop are you?

Backing out to a search box, I type **hypoxia** and 3,619 matches come back, most of them medical in orientation, many of which I've read, or at least printed. A new one from dartmouth.edu: **A longitudinal study found an increased risk of schizophrenia in individuals subjected to episodes of hypoxia.**

I bring up sexdoc.com: **Sexual hypoxia is rarely intentional murder...** Such "edge behavior," the doc recommends, should be practiced only in the presence of a trained and trusted partner. I scroll down, find *teensmother.com,* click on **more like this**, and look to the priest in his cubicle. No response. I open a Word screen and write in my best Spanish: "Father? Are you there? Could these perversions be another example of humans getting it wrong? Making the beautiful ugly? I mean, just because God allowed the Inquisitors to burn children on the steps of this very building doesn't mean Heaven is empty. Does it?" I look to the cubicle expecting something. Penance, absolution, rage, something. But the ghostly father has lost his way, and his eyes stay fixed on the cathode ray.

Doesn't matter. I just have to get drunk enough for a coroner to call the leap a fall.

Logging out, I go upstairs to the Cathedral, wandering eventually into the Capilla de Mariscal, where four Sisters of the Side Wound watch over the net bags that contain their earthly possessions while two nuns with buckets and sponges pepper them with questions they don't understand. The Sisters use the Capilla as a sort of base camp because it is a rarely visited backwater of the Cathedral, stuck in a dark corner behind the Sacrista de los Calices. But today, with the Cardinal coming, the nuns are making a bid to reclaim their dominion in full. The reja protecting the altarpiece bears a bronze crest depicting *Christ placed in the Tomb.* The work wears a dull patina except for the side wound, which has been polished to a brilliant gloss by the lips and fingers of the Sisters. I touch the petals of the spear wound as I walk by, drawing stares from both the Sisters and the nuns.

A soft glow spreads from the doors of the Sacrista de los Calices framing Goya's painting of Justina and Rufina, putting a sidebar halo around the patron saints. The painting is little different from all the other paintings of the two virgins in the Cathedral. The girls are depicted before their torture, the pagan idol broken on the ground before them, earthenware and palm fronds in their hands, the Guadalquivir and the Giralda in the background. The only license Goya takes is the lion he puts at the bare feet of Rufina. The big cat anoints her toes with his tongue, his face misconstrued like a flounder's, his rump and curling tail growing from the top of his head. Perhaps Picasso walked by the painting as a boy, his eyes passing over this curiously distorted lion which would transmigrate years later into bulls, and guitars, and the faces of women. Who knows?

There are rows of jewel-encrusted communion cups in the Sacrista. Rows of gold reliquaries containing the bones of saints and splinters of the True Cross. I remember something from my own childhood: *How beautiful are thy feet, O prince's daughter! The joints of thy thighs are like jewels, the work of a cunning craftsman. Thy navel is like a round goblet, which wanteth not liquor.*

God had been force-fed me by an adoptive-mother, but it was not this Catholic God of painting and sculpture and precious metalwork. Our Holy Roller Lord was embodied by the Word. *In the beginning was the Word,* and the Word was the King James Bible. Sometime during the self-pollination stage of my catechism, I came across the Song of Solomon and the above words stuck.

Some men ejaculate when hung.

Here's a word:

Rapture.

APRIL WOKE ME reciting a dirty poem with hand motions, touching her dime-sized nipples, hooking her fingers under her cotton-clad pudendum, finally poking her anus with her thumb.

"Milk! Cheese! Wemonade! Awound the corner fudge is made!" She ran away cackling. I squinted past my tent flaps at the yard, littered with beer cans. A couple of lawn torches still burned.

"Quite an internship, huh?" Dr. Abbott drank coffee in a lawn chair in front of my tent. "First field lesson: Never try to keep up with Duval when he's drinking."

I'd read Abbott's book and agreed with him that there were plenty of ways for Europeans to get to the American interior in the mid 1500s that did not include the lost Templar fleet Duval put so much stock in. Otherwise, I disliked the professor.

"Where is he? Duval?"

"Tennessee. West Virginia," Abbott shrugged. "Depends on which way he went."

I recalled riding on Duval's motorcycle, going for more beer, having my arms around him, breathing rushing air, asphalt and foliage blurring in my peripheral vision, the flame of some foundry flapping against the sky.

April sat under a tree, amusing herself with a red brindle dog. "If-yer-happy-and-yew-know-it-nod-yer-head," she sang, pumping the poor animal's snout. None of the others were up.

"I'm gonna take a walk," I said. I was glad Abbott didn't volunteer to go along.

Following the Red to the conflux of the Tug, I turned up the hollow and walked the quarter of a mile to the Gohan homestead. Though the trailer had been dragged out years ago, it was not hard to find the site. There were three apple trees gone wild from lack of pruning but planted in a row, and around the place where the house had stood were blades of iris in bloom, the planting of Earl's wife, Belva. And there was Belva's grave. And Earl's.

Earl had been a fool to try to farm this narrow strip of land that lay in shade until ten in the morning. He was trying to get away from the world, trying to find a place where he could hear the voice of the Lord and it was amazing he'd made it work as long as he did before the world found him, before his only daughter turned up pregnant and he threw her out.

That signaled the unraveling. His sons left and his wife died and Earl hung on alone, listening to whatever whispers came from the forest until one winter day they told him to lie down one last time over Belva and shoot himself twice in the head with a .22 revolver.

I sat on a cement block at the base of an apple tree wondering what I thought I'd find in Kentucky. The ground was littered with cigarette butts. Pall Malls. Beneath last fall's leaves, a nub of flesh colored plastic peeked out. Barbie was nude and headless but otherwise holding up well under the ravages of time. A month later, when I left to go back to Ohio, I gave the doll to April, who already possessed that lopsided smile too big for her face, already lush and wet like a slice of watermelon.

I ORDER SANGRIA in the first air-conditioned café I come to.

Postcards: To Sharon Widdy, a photo of an Altamira Bison. "Having a great time! No bull!" To Ron Norton, who's feeding my dog, a shot of Gibraltar with a Union Jack superimposed. "Having a bloody fine time." To Mom, a reproduction of *The Guardian Angel* from the Cathedral gift shop. "Having a great time," I write. Then, forcing myself, "I love you." And another reproduction card, *The Little Ancient One*. I look at her while the Sangria works. She does not look heavenward and she does not look pious. She looks to the floor as though embarrassed. She was brought to the old Mosque after Christian reconquest in 1248 and miraculously survived the earthquake of 1356. When the Cathedral was built over the rubble, she was reinstalled and subsequent generations of artists began surrounding her with gaudy clutter — Baroque gold-leaf and garish Rococo cherubs. Over her head, angels hold a silver crown, added in 1929 when artists should have known better. Still the simple peasant girl shines through like an uncut diamond, keeping the integrity of her virginity and her poverty, as no artist has been brazen enough to reach onto her body and add so much as a ring. But she is assuredly rich with the lustful excesses of the invisible lover kneeling before her, into whose face she looks, surprised and shocked and secretly pleased that he would want her in a way she never suspected anyone could. That innocent surprise can only show itself once, for once it is known it is gone. And that is what is so profound about this little peasant girl in the throes of Immaculate Conception, this Little Ancient One.

After working off an ROTC obligation, I took discharge in Germany and spent a year stumbling through Europe, lost, sometimes unaware if the ruins I surveyed were Greek or Roman, first traveling with an Irish woman, eventually taking up with an Israeli girl. It was with her that I first wandered through the Cathedral of Seville and into the Biblioteca Columbina. Dr. Abbott had said the answer to the Black Jackson riddle was probably there, buried in the uncatalogued material from that dark era when Spain simultaneously conducted holocausts in America and Europe. Through glass display cases I inspected samples of archaic Spanish script and moved on, resigned that any secrets residing in the locked vaults of the Cathedral were not about to reveal themselves to me. A climbing accident in the Alps finally sent me back to the states, where I eventually drifted west, ending up working as a waiter at Paradise Inn on Mt. Rainier, climbing on my days off.

It was a newspaper clip from mother that brought me back to Kentucky. Duval had ridden his bike into the Gorge. The article said alcohol was a factor.

I told myself it was to alleviate destitution that I offered Trinh Jackson three hundred dollars—all that I had—for the pick of a newborn litter of pit bulls.

April sat in the straw with the puppies all around her, sullen, distracted, not interested in talking.

"Which is your favorite?" I asked. She was unwilling to even look up.

"I don't got one," she said, brushing the runt from her lap.

We were quiet awhile. "You know who I am?"

133

She shrugged, then nodded. The runt climbed into her lap again and she let him stay this time.

"My first day back at school this boy on the bus named Mitchell said his grandpa said Daddy weren't no Indian at all but just a half-ass nigger and that my Mommy was a just a half-assed gook and that all I was was a niggergook an ..." she swallowed, trying not to cry, "... an he started saying it over and over again. Niggergook, niggergook. An then the others started saying it over and over and over again and again and laughing at me..."

That's when it came, forcing its way out of her in trembles and grimaces and little tics and, finally, tears.

She sat there in front of me shaking and shuddering, and I didn't know what to do. My hands went out but they only comforted the air around her, that fundamental Protestantism that had been forced into me making me afraid to touch. But April flew into my arms at the sign of this opening. She slammed her tiny frame into my torso and squeezed my neck with all her might. She loosened a torrent of tears on my shoulder and I found myself rubbing her back up and down like I was pumping a well until it was all out of her.

I've written this scene over and over again. I've written about moving my face through her mane, getting lost trying to find her ear, becoming intoxicated by the scent of her unwashed hair.

"April, listen to me," I whispered. "Listen. People like that boy say those things because they're jealous. They look at you and they're jealous because it's plain to see that you're so uncommon. You sparkle like a jewel. Anyone can see that. Anyone can see that you're royalty. That you're a princess. A princess of a lost tribe. And some people just can't stand that, so they try to crush you down into the same hole they're in. But don't you let them. And this dog? This dog is never going to fight. He's going to live better than most people, April, and you're going to be able to see him whenever you want," I heard myself say, "because I'm moving down here."

She pulled away and wiped her eyes. "You *are?*"

She was nine then.

FROM THE TOP of the giralda, the shaman looks like a bug lying on his back in the shadow of an orange tree, his fingers dipped in the flow of one of the tiny streams running from the Fountain of the Well. Activity surrounds him. Sisters of the Side Wound huddle in conversation. They check his pulse and change his diaper. A black baby runs across the patio naked, his pert little spigot pointing the way, oblivious to the stares of the nuns sweeping the bricks. The Sisters pick up the stretcher and walk away wearily, the shaman's arm dangling, wet fingers extended as if still seeking water.

A masonry arrow inlaid in the bricks on the courtyard points to Mecca. It would not be unusual for a man as drunk as I to fall on that arrow.

I try to keep my head, direct my thoughts, concentrate on the patio below.

When the Moors took Seville in 711 they destroyed the Arian temple of the Visigoths and dug a well on the spot as a token of contempt, making the high place low. Around the well they planted oranges and dug a network of rivulets to irrigate the grove. Centuries later Yusuf-ben Yacub built his Great Mosque around the grove, raising the Giralda to call the faithful to take their ablutions in the streams of the fountain and pray beneath the oranges. When the Spaniards defeated the Moors and raised their great Cathedral, they kept, for reasons unclear, the Islamic Giralda, the Garden of Oranges, and the Fountain of the Well.

It is three in the afternoon in Seville, and hot. It's been twenty-eight days since I was with April . 672 hours. Well over 40,000 minutes.

"I'm here to try out for the Climb Club!" she announced that day at the Furnace Ruin. "I'm joining next fall, as if you didn't guess. If you're still the sponsor. You *are* going to sponsor Climb Club next year, aren't you?" She turned and pulled onto the wall of the furnace without waiting for an answer. "The chalk kind of shows the way don't it? Look. I'm as tall as you now. And now… now I'm taller. And this, this is where it gets tricky, huh? I mean this is where the chalk starts to thin out. Looks hard." She made another move and somehow stayed on the rock. "But it's not."

Her hips jutted out. Manners should have made me step back, but I leaned into her instead. Nothing. I leaned closer and picked it up. Just a tinge, a hint. I pulled back. Repulsion? No. Then what? I leaned in again. Closer. Lingering. Aware that she was watching. Closer still, taking in the full nose of her, the musky malodor hovering somewhere between nasty and delicious.

How to explain it? Once I had several hundred words comparing her to the bouquet of a fine wine, full of complexities and complications, one flavor hiding behind another. In a later rewrite, I went Zen, finding the cycle of existence in her scent, the death that evolves into fertility. In short, I've invented a number of metaphors and similes to distinguish myself from a dog in heat. But that afternoon at the Furnace Ruin, the region of sentience and syntax went dark in my brain. It was as if the whole world condensed into that fragrant blue seam, like the salinity of that damp fabric was a nine-volt battery on my tongue. I knew no law. No taboo. I took her in my hands and for a moment thought she resisted, though I didn't care. Then I knew she was only finding purchase in my bones, climbing me like a rock, pulling herself onto me, riding me. And I went willingly. Wanting to drown in her, be taken in. Live inside and slip this skin.

I look at my watch. It's 3:16 in Spain. 9:16 in Kentucky, still cool in the hills. Perhaps she is waking, maybe already eating Fruit Loops in front of the TV, sitting on the carpet, slouched against the couch, knees propped up, feet turned in on each other pigeon-toed. Maybe the dogs are with her, putting their wet noses to her lean hip, sensing the coming of her fecund cycle.

I lost consciousness at the Furnace Ruin. Or maybe I died. When I came to, April was straddling me, the heel of her hand pumping my chest, her mouth on mine, blowing breath back into my lungs. She pulled away and her lips were crimson. Crimson from my lips.

"OhmygodIthoughtIkilledyou!" she pulled up my t-shirt and wiped her mouth. "Gross!" she had said. "How embarrassing!"

I stare down at the arrow that points to Mecca. It's just after nine in Kentucky, still cool in the hills. Perhaps she is eating Fruit Loops in front of the TV, feet turned in pigeon-toed. Maybe the dogs are with her, putting their noses to her hip. Or, maybe, she is at her keyboard.

DO YOU HAVE a digital camera? Dawson wants to know. I think it might be wise for you to open a new e-mail account too if we are going to talk about your modeling career.

Wut do u think of the nu pics I posted???? April answers. N sure I have a camera!, u want me 2 take pics of myself? u want my home address or n e thing? b sure 2 sign my guest book!!!

The site has somehow registered 463 hits. There is the picture of her in my chair, and there are two new pictures. In the first, she is six, wearing an Easter bonnet and holding a basket with a big Hershey's candy bar in it. The other photo is her favorite. She is in her track uniform and her hair is washed and curled and some creepy photographer, who drives from school to school touching girls on the cheek, has put her head at an unnatural angle.

You there, Babe? Dawson writes. **What's that you're holding in your hand?**

An email from April hits the screen: its a pole for polevalting its a new sport 4 girls n KY and im the only 1 n my school that does it i did 6, 6,, last year and made the varsity team as an 8th grader that guy who took the pic of me n the chair got me n2 it cuz he sad it wud b a way 2 get a scholarship he got me nterested n running wen he used 2 jog passed my house w/ his dog wen i wuz a little kid he never nu this but i used to sit by the window and w8 4 him he turned around at a fone poll just a little past my house n id run w/ him n every couple of weeks wed run 2 the next poll n so on n so on i started running JVXC wen i was only a 6 grader n i wuz usually pretty far back cuz i wuz so much younger then the other girls but he used 2 come 2 the meets n whistle real loud wen he saw me n i would start running real hard cause he wuz watching n i never want 2 let him down never n f i have im sorry

I become aware of the priest at my shoulder. "We are closing," he says. "The Cardinal is here and you must leave."

137

I turn back to the words on the screen. it wuz like wen I wuz having problems n school cause i hated 2 read and he started reading Shakespeer w/ me he sad the old words were best n said the most but i still thot the whole thing wuz dum but i got the movie w/ Leonardo and i memorized the words just so i could act like i wuz reading so he woodnt think he wuz wasting his time on me so he would start caring about me as much as i care about him but i got cot up n it, u c i got cot up in the story and coodnt stop watching it cuz every time i wanted it 2 end differently i still do want it 2 end differently because its not enuff its just not enuff theres so much more 2 do.

i wish u felt as bad as i do goddam u i have a stomachache n a headache nd n ill divining soul f thou hast a remedy - please - b not so long 2 speak

I need air. I need to leave the library and run for miles and sweat the tobacco and alcohol and craziness from my body. Then maybe I can think. Then maybe I can figure out what to do.

Sangria writhes in the pit of my belly, spinning, thrashing, gathering momentum, grand mal coming on. I have to get out of the library, get out of the Cathedral. Stumbling up the stairs my vision constricts and I find myself in a crowd, people against me, pushing me, breathing on me. The Cardinal is in the Cathedral and I am being carried along by the throng, pressed toward the Sacristy against my will.

The Cardinal is ninety. His face is half paralyzed, his hands palsied, and he sits on a kind of high bench attended by priests who distribute wine to an interminable line of communicants. The Cardinal holds a host aloft occasionally, breaks it, then motions the line to move faster. Come on, he gestures. Let's get this over with. But then the line stops. Two policemen have halted the Sisters of the Side Wound just as they are about to approach the altar with the stretcher bearing their shaman. A priest whispers in the Cardinal's ear but the old man pushes him away and signals the line to start moving again. Another priest bends to whisper, gesticulating plaintively, but the Cardinal cuts him off and waves the Sisters forward. Still they are held back, as the Shaman's body is showing signs of rigor mortis. The Cardinal struggles to stand, then falls back on the bench ranting. The priest shrugs and the Sisters are allowed to come forward. The coiling force rises in my spine, pulsating surges of light. I push through the crowd. I must get outside before my skull erupts.

There is a downpour on the Patio de los Naranjos. Rain hits the bricks and turns to steam. Water catapults off the leaves of orange trees and flies back to the sky. The patio rocks like a boat in a tempest.

Hold on, I tell myself. Hold on. This will pass. Earthquake or storm or grand mal seizure, this will pass and I'll find a way out. Just because there is fog, the door has not disappeared. It is there somewhere. The Door of Pardons. So I hold on. As water like the Colorado leaps from the Fountain of the Well, I hold on.

Revelation

Pearl's shoestrings are knotted and I cannot untie them. The strings are bound so tight they seem melded. The girl sighs and wags her foot, further frustrating my efforts to remove her shoe.

The shoes are black and white saddle oxfords and I've watched them age since her first day at Calvary Academy. The shoes were shiny and stiff then, and she stood up in them to say she hated her mother, all lawyers, John Walsh, and *America's Most Wanted.* But mostly, she said, she hated each and every one of the boys and girls gathered in the chapel for Prayer Power Hour. I said I'd ask God to forgive her, then she said something else that, I told her, was about the worst thing a person possibly could say. She said she was glad I thought so, and said it again, this time suggesting that I play an active role in the scenario.

"Stop her!" cried Annie Hooper. "She's got the devil in her! She's got the devil in her!" and ran from the room with her hands over her ears.

"Don't you know who this Pearl is?" I asked Reverend Endicott when he returned from one of his forbidden auto excursions. But the Reverend answered only with that otherworldly rheum that had come over him since his stroke.

Of course he knew. Everyone knew. She had first been a face on flyers taped to convenience store windows, followed fast by local TV at six and eleven, then on network news and, finally, around the clock on FOX and MSNBC. But even then, after her weight and height and the scar on her knee had been broadcast across America, did anyone really know her?

"Why this girl?" Jessee Sharpton had asked on *Hannity and Colmes.* "Why not Latisha Jones or Shondra Johnson?" And for a day or two, those other missing girls had been featured as well. Then the coverage crept back to Pearl, tentatively at first like an errant lover begging forgiveness, then, as ratings came in, with unabashed devotion. Forget Sharpton. It was going to be all Pearl, all the time. There was home video of Pearl in pigtails and painted-on freckles, chased across a stage by a boy in a wolf suit. Pearl clearing hurdles and sprinting around the turn. Pearl doing a cartwheel on a balance beam. And always, like a benediction, Pearl emerging from some Appalachian lake, arms and legs slick like the water had just birthed her, American Venus in a two-piece.

"These slices of her life," a TV psychologist said, "have taken on the power of myth. They mean so much more than they seem to say on the surface. Seeing them forces us to confront the fact that we have a hole in our collective soul. *A Pearl shaped hole.*"

Then she was seen kicking and screaming, her hair cut short and dyed, being carried from a California motel, fighting her baffled FBI saviors with feline ferocity. TV shrinks jumped on the Stockholm syndrome bandwagon: "We should not think of her," they said, "as anything but a victim."

So Pearl was returned to her mother and, after repatriation to public school failed, was enrolled at Calvary Academy, whereupon she entered my Christian Awareness class.

The girl smirked at creation.

"Come *on.* Evolution is more believable than *that.*"

She sneered at Abraham's willingness to obey God.

"He heard voices telling him to kill his kid? Wasn't there a woman in Texas like that?"

But her greatest scorn was saved for the virgin birth.

"Joseph must have been a real moron to buy that one," she laughed.

"Why don't you just shut your dumb mouth," Heather Sisselman said. "We all *know* you aren't a virgin. We *know* what you did."

"You can't imagine what I did," Pearl answered. "You might know the places he took me, but you *can't imagine* what we did."

"Some parents wonder why she was allowed to enroll," I confided in Reverend Endicott later that day. "Some of these parents have pledged a great deal to the building fund and they question what purpose she serves among us."

"These parents?" the Reverend said, pivoting on his cane. "The ones with the money who question this child's purpose? They are the Pharisees of our time, Paul. They are the comfortable clergy who crucified Christ."

I was shocked. Reverend Endicott had married my parents and buried my grandparents. He had baptized me by total immersion in running water the summer I turned thirteen. But he had changed.

Since emerging from the hospital, his sermons had become incoherent ramblings in which he laughed at the coming of glory one moment and wept for the fate of the damned the next. For Endicott, the Lord had truly become Alpha and Omega in a single breath, the creator and destroyer in the self-same thought. Extemporaneous emanations of his muddled memory swirled in a biblical mishmash, the Book of Daniel blending with Revelations, Isaiah sluicing into St. John. Now and then, a fragment of *Amazing Grace* or *Just as I Am* would abruptly burst forth from a sermon just like the sun sometimes erupted through the stained glass, striking the pulpit with such awed effect that those in the pews would turn to the damascened windows to see whatever it was that he saw. *Just as I am, without one plea. I once was blind, but now I see.*

When Reverend Endicott was admitted to the hospital at Christmas, I took over his duties, and discovered, in the bottom drawer of his desk, the secret of his forbidden drives.

HE HAD BEEN going to the library where he had evidently searched back issues of *The Menifee Monitor*, finding and photocopying articles about Pearl and the man who would eventually abduct her. The kidnapper, a prominent physician, had been able to keep things quiet at first. Though Pearl's mother had gotten a restraining order, Dr. Logan Sutherland managed to keep his name out of the paper until after his first arrest. Then, on the courthouse steps, after posting bail, he denied everything. His relationship with the unnamed, under-age female in question had been strictly professional. He was, after all, a doctor. True, they had on occasion met while bicycling on rural roads near her home — yes, even after the restraining order had been issued — but those meetings had been coincidental and innocent. He didn't know why people said the horrible things they did. He didn't know why they spread such awful rumors. There were some places in the human heart he would never understand, he said. Places that were perhaps beyond understanding. But he looked forward to clearing his name in court. And his wife stood beside him and held his hand for the sake of the photographer.

"The idea of a man like Logan being interested in a child is ludicrous," a colleague from the hospital was quoted as saying. "Dr. Sutherland is the victim of a backwoods witch-hunt. The situation is nothing less than Kafkaesque."

Kafkaesque. That's what he said. Kafkaesque in Kentucky.

But that first article opened the floodgates. Thereafter, an article appeared in *The Monitor* almost daily, for the doctor had hired a lawyer who loved to see his own name in print. The attorney called witnesses liars one day, inciting a response from those witnesses the next, whereupon the lawyer complained to reporters that his client was being tried in the press, evoking a counter charge from the prosecutor's office. And each article contained the same retelling of the lurid allegations. For the local media's part, the charade of protecting the anonymity of a minor was upheld even as details such as age, the name of the school she attended, and the neighborhood in which she lived, were published repeatedly, easily identifying Pearl to all who knew her.

Then, one May afternoon a week before his trial was to begin, the cardiologist cleaned out his bank accounts and parked on a street near Pearl's school. By most accounts, she resisted when he pulled her into the BMW.

From an archive service, Endicott had purchased newscast footage as well as some of the photographs Sutherland took during his travels with Pearl. Pearl smiling at Mystery Hill. Pearl feeding from a paper bag at Mt. Rushmore. Pearl posing with a llama in Georgia. I held the photos in my hand. I spread them out on the dying minister's desk, one next to the other. It was like Pearl and her middle-aged paramour were trying to create some kind of, well, family vacation.

Then, on the Internet, I discovered many of the same images, some of which purported to be pornographic pictures the physician had taken, but which were actually Pearl's digitally decapitated head dissonantly pasted onto some other girl's neck. Most of these creations were botched jobs, but one in particular was exceptionally well done, I thought, in that the host body appeared to belong to a girl about Pearl's age and was posed to artfully accept Pearl's over-the-shoulder glance, which I recognized from a photograph the doctor had taken on Mt. Baker. I printed all the images of Pearl I found online, regardless of how prurient or poorly done, and added them to the minister's own collection in the bottom drawer of his desk.

If the congregation knew of this growing stack of material they would call for blood, I realized, be it Endicott's or mine, and that, I told myself, is where they would be wrong. America's fascination with Pearl's meandering odyssey was a cultural phenomenon worthy of study. Our collective interest was purely sociological. But the truth is, I couldn't turn away, and though I told myself every afternoon, 'today I will do something else. I will read or go for a hike,' the Reverend's darkened study drew me like the Sirens' song every afternoon after all the students and teachers were gone for the day. I reread articles and court transcripts. I scoured the World Wide Web for newly concocted images, the possession of which was perhaps a violation of law. Nevertheless, my research continued. It grew.

I began positioning myself in the hall between periods to watch her walk by, trying to imagine what she had that would make a man of education, a man with a respected position in the community, forsake everything, throw it all away, and destroy himself. I looked for whatever that thing was and told myself I couldn't find it in her. So I concluded it wasn't in Pearl at all but in some secret thing that lurked in the man — the Doctor — something dark and deep and unsatisfied. So my attention turned to Sutherland, to the sad image of the deer-in-the-headlights as he had been lead back and forth between the courtroom and jail, in handcuffs and shackles and blaze orange pajamas, his hair disheveled, and it was plain to see he had no idea what had hit him.

143

One day, there was a knock on the door. Miss Mauzer had caught Pearl smoking in the restroom.

PEARL SAT BEFORE me, limbs crossed.

"I don't want to do this," I said, waving the demerit slip.

"Don't let it bother you too much. It's not like it *means* anything. I mean it doesn't mean anything to *me*, and I'm the one it's supposed to scare, right? But I'm *not* scared, see. What's five demerits? Give me a billion. A trillion. What the hell *is* a demerit anyway? It's nothing. It's like your stupid religion where you sit around doing nothing waiting to die so you can be rewarded for sitting around doing nothing. Well you don't get rewarded for that. You get *bored*, and that's a *punishment*. Then you get old and ugly and finally die and all that happens then is you fall asleep. Except you don't dream. And, oh yeah. You never wake up."

My face flushed. "So nothing has meaning?"

"Did *I* say that? No, *you* said that because you need something to say and nothing else came to mind. The world is *full* of meaning. It's just not any of … *this!*" And she gestured so that I was not sure if she meant the bookcases, the diplomas on the wall, our conversation, or even myself. I thought of those months she'd spent with Sutherland, bouncing around the map like a pinball, hiding in the herd of tourists, driving for twenty hours at a stretch, then laying up for weeks at a time, buying cars from undocumented workers, swapping license plates in parking lots, staying a couple of motel rooms ahead of Geraldo Rivera.

"Look," she said, leaning forward. "Logan was no braver than you. And he had a hell of a lot more to lose."

"What?" I said. "What are you saying?"

"Just that I'll be hitting the road soon. If you want to come, that's fine. I need someone older to take care of things. But if you want to stay here, that's okay too. Just when the time comes, you either jump on board or get out of my way."

"What?" I said. "What?"

She smiled. It was the same lopsided smile I saw in the photograph at Mt. Baker.

I LOCKED THE minister's study and took refuge in the closet that was my old office. I purged the offending files from my computer's recollection and prayed that God would do the same. Into my own sea of forgetfulness I tried to cast those remembered images of Pearl. Still, morning after morning, those banished memories furtively washed ashore upon waking, drenching me with guilt.

So I stayed in my office during the day, minding administrative minutia. Then the bell would ring to change classes and I would glance at the clock and know what stretch of hallway Pearl would be walking, her books against her chest, her eyes defiant. Outside, layers of forgetful snow covered the churchyard, keeping the graves of my lineage insulated. I was immune to whatever disease had taken Doctor Sutherland, I told myself. The cloth from which he was cut contained scarlet threads that were not part of my constitution. My interest in Pearl was a passing fancy with fame, a mildly embarrassing need to associate myself with notoriety.

Then it was March and Reverend Endicott suddenly stood before me, pale and thin, bones under skin as transparent as a newly hatched sparrow's, veins climbing those bones like winter's wisteria on a white washed trellis, cold blue tendrils branching at his temples, reaching out over his bald head and touching the sunken sockets of his eyes.

The deacons came to me. It was a pity what was happening to Reverend Endicott, they said, but it couldn't go on much longer. He had fallen into doctrinal fallacy, bordering on heresy. He was no longer a fit minister for such an old and prestigious congregation. While they wanted to avoid a scene at all costs, they wanted to know, when the time came, as it surely was, would I be ready? Would I be willing?

Lent came. The great blank white receded from the hollows, then from the hills, leaving brown earth, which was in turn threatened by splotches of green. Reverend Endicott hung on, seeming to gain power even as his body shrank beneath his clothes, his voice becoming high and thin like mountain air. On Palm Sunday, he announced that Calvary Academy would observe a Maundy Thursday foot washing. The congregation was invited as well.

THOUGH STILL FOUND in the dustier corners of our doctrine, foot washing had long ago lost fashion. Dating from a time and place when people traveled over dusty roads in sandals, to wash another's feet was to put them above you, to humble yourself as Mary Magdalene did when she washed Jesus' feet with perfume and dried them with her hair, or as Jesus Himself did for His disciples at the Last Supper, hours before His arrest. I hoped Endicott would forget about it like he forgot my name and the days of the week. He didn't.

Doddering and breathless, he spoke to the students, seated alphabetically by homeroom, about the freedom and release obtained through submission and bondage. He told them damnation was necessary for redemption to occur, that sin was the collateral that gave salvation coin. He told them if they hoped to find themselves they must lose themselves first. Lose themselves completely, like Israelites wandering the wilderness. Like a lamb far from the flock. Only then, will God come looking for you. Only then will He reveal Himself.

Endicott came down from the pulpit and knelt before Martha Abbott, removing her sensible shoes and washing her feet. He handed the pitcher back to me shakily, then dried her with a towel. Failing to rise under his own power, I took him under his arms and tried to lift him, but he was all dead weight, his legs providing no lift. He felt as if he was about to pull apart under the rib cage, so I lowered him, as he indicated I should, and he proceeded to crawl to Ryan Adams. He pulled the laces of Ryan's Nikes and managed to wash the timid boy. Then on to Lucas Auden, then Judd Baldwin, who didn't get the message and should have showered, then Jesse Bierce, then Miss Stephens, who hid on the lee side of her considerable girth one very small Pearl Bradstreet.

"Paul," Endicott gasped. "I've finished the race. I can't go on. Now it is up to you."

PEARL'S SADDLE OXFORDS have lost their original distinction, the white and black headed for the same shade of scuffed gray. She's just a girl, I tell myself. She has no special power within her. I'm a modern man, not some superstitious brute believing in fertility talismans and fetish objects. Pearl is just a girl. She is representative of nothing. She is not a symbol.

Pearl's shoe says "hush" as I pull it from her heel. The warmth of her foot wafts around my face and I hold my breath to shut her out, deny her entry.

I am a modern man. I am dependable. A man to be counted on. Stable. Trusted. Pearl has no power over me.

Then I breathe Pearl in not because I want to, or desire her more than I have ever desired anything in my life, but because I must. Because I'm a man and a man must breathe. I breathe the breath of Pearl's flesh and it smells faintly of yeast. Of fermentation and warm bread.

She is no Goddess.

I do not serve her above all others.

I do not worship her just because I kneel and tremble.

Your Lolita

MITCHELL WAS THE first one to recognize me.

I knew someone would figure out who I was sooner or later and it makes sense it would be a lowlife prick like Mitchell.

You probably wouldn't remember Mitchell. There's not a lot to remember. He rode my bus and made my life miserable when I was in the eighth grade. Other than that he was just another hilljack hanging out in the halls with bad skin and a John Deere hat.

I was on stage when he recognized me. Swinging around the old pole. He's greatly changed, Mitchell, having lost his teeth somehow, but there was no mistaking those pig eyes.

"Yer name ain't Lolita!" he yelled. (Like, *Duh!* No shit, Sherlock.) "Yer name's *D.B. Wells!* Hey everybody, this yere's *D.B. Wells!* 'Member her? She's dyed her hair but hit's her!"

Well that was it for the pole show. I headed for the scratch box but he came waddling along beside me. "Hey D.B.! D.B.! 'Member me? Mitchell? Look D.B.! Look!" He took out his billfold. "I gots some munny! I want yew t' dance fer me! Over there! In one of them lil booths!"

"Where's your teeth, creep?"

"Hey now. If yew don' dance fer me, why I'll ... I'll *tell yer boss!*"

"You won't have far to walk, Hoss," Gordy said. "Hit the road."

"Huh?" Mitchell said stupidly, not comprehending.

"Leave the premises immediately," Gordy said. "I want you out of here right now."

"Yer throwin' *me* out?" Mitchell looked around like he expected someone to defend his right of free speech in a tittie bar. "But she's *D.B. Wells.* You 'member 'bout her. It was on the television all 'bout how her an' this guy..."

He was still trying to give the Cliff's Notes version when he was shoved into the parking lot, the management of Gentleman Jim's Nude Revue knowing the value of a girl who can scratch her ear with her big toe. But I'm sure old Mitch is back in Massieville this very moment, telling everybody what D.B. is up to in the big city of Newport, Kentucky.

Cluck, cluck, cluck, their tongues go. They *knowd* it was bound to happen. Bad seed, see. Bad blood. But it ain't *all* her fault. That *man* ruined her. And he *knowd* better. He coulda stopped if he wanted to. He took her innocence an' kept *note*books about it all. *Awful* stuff. She didn't have no chance once't that got out. But we all *knowd* she'd end up like that. We all *knowd* it.

But won't one person in that pigshit town raise a voice in our defense? Won't someone say, sure they did some shit, but weren't they always true *to each other*? Won't someone put the brakes on the bad-mouthing and say, "Hold on now. That girl's barely outta her teens. So she ain't ended up any way, *yet*."?

Won't anyone say that?

Nope. Not if I know Massieville.

ACTUALLY, MITCHELL WASN'T even the first person to recognize me. There's this other guy with gray hair who knows who I am, too. Gordy says he always calls ahead the day before to see when I'm scheduled. And sure enough, when I come out on stage, there he is in the corner booth. That's kind of funny because the corner booth has the worst lighting of all the booths and most guys like as much light as they can get. So I figure he was somebody who didn't want to be seen in a place like Gentleman Jim's.

At first he just sat there and drank diet Sprite and watched me go through my stage grind. Whenever I would go over to see if I could get a little table action going he'd just start stammering and throw a tip down and leave all of a sudden like he thought he was going to get an STD or something. Then he started coming in a little more frequently and after awhile, loosened up enough to buy a real drink.

The next time he came in he bought two drinks.

That was when he bought his first dance. Then he started coming in more often. Sometimes two days in a row on weekends, buying dance after dance, only from me, dropping hundreds of bucks, just sitting there while

I went through the same moves over and over and over, dancing on a three by four foot table top being about as limiting as trying to write a haiku. After a while he would get up, thank me, take my hand, and press fifty or sixty bucks into my palm. Other than that, he never touched me, or suggested that I touch him, or asked me to screw him for X amount of dollars, or so on or so on. So I was always glad as hell to see *him* sitting in the corner booth. He was no trouble and he was a big tipper.

"Watch him," Gordy said one night after closing when we were counting our loot. "He drives rental cars from the airport."

"Check it out!" this black chick called The Raven said. "Gordy's a detective! He's a regular Columbo! *'He drives rental cars from the airport.'"*

Gordy scowled. "All I'm saying is an airplane ride is a hell of a trip just to sniff a shaved snatch."

"Why Gordon," I said, "what a poetic turn of phrase. I just love the alliteration."

"Don't pull that shit," he said. "I'm just looking out for you is all. I'm just telling you so you'll be ready when he gets funny."

"Hey everybody, Gordy's gone sweet on Lolita!" quoth The Raven. "He's turning red so it must be true!"

SO ONE DAY the gray guy from the airport was there and he was more nervous than usual. He seemed to want to talk. I mean in between the dances. So I was telling him about the girls who work at Gentleman Jim's and what total bitches they are and so on, but Gordy kept walking by looking at his watch so I said, "Listen, I like to chat as much as anyone but I gotta produce some of the long green if you know what I mean, so if I don't drop my pants and dance every once in awhile I gotta vacate the booth. That's what Gordy's watch watching is about, if you were wondering."

"What if I paid you and you didn't dance?" he said. "What if I paid you thirty-five dollars—what?—every five or six minutes? and instead of dancing, we just talked? That's not against the rules is it? Here. Here's two hundred dollars. Will that do for a half-hour? Take it. Show it to the manager if that's what you need to do, but put it away so we don't have to think about it anymore. And you can put your things on too if you want."

I did.

"So?" I said. "What do you wanna talk about?"

He fidgeted around in his coat pocket and I could tell he was nervous and it made me nervous, too, like he was going to jerk out a blade or something and I was ready to beat a path to the nearest exit when he pulls out a copy of *Yemassee*.

"This story you wrote," he said. "It doesn't have a real ending does it? I mean it's like all those other stories you've published. They're good stories but I was wondering … and some other people were wondering … if you might consider putting it all together and writing the whole story. You know. The whole thing. Not just the bits and pieces you dribble out to these literary magazines. I mean, there is some interest in that." He handed me his card. "There's a figure on the back," he said.

"*Advance against* royalties =," he had written on the card, and then a number.

"And you've just been sitting on this the whole time you've been coming here? Get a big kick out of that, did you? Watching me humiliate myself while this offer was on the table. No. I was *on* the table. This was *under* the table. And how about them airline tickets? Did that come out of my money? And all of those dances you bought? The whole time I was shaking my ass in your face I was actually paying for it myself, huh? And the five dollar diet Sprites and all the booze. Even the cost of this little chat. It all comes out of my money, right?"

"No," he said, and he looked like he could cry. "That's not the way it is. I didn't plan it … I can't explain…. But that's not the way it is."

He put his fingers through his hair and looked so exhausted that he reminded me a little of you when we were near the end and you knew there wasn't much more left. So I felt a little sorry for him at first, but I've learned to resist that emotion. It's usually a wasted one.

"More," I said, throwing the card back at him. "I want more. I want enough so I can quit dancing and have the same standard of living. I'm not going to sacrifice for this. I've already sacrificed too much. So get me more."

THE COPS TOOK the laptop and all your notebooks. I tried to get them back but all I got were smirks.

"They're evidence," I was told at the DA's office. (First thing, let's kill all the lawyers!)

But here's a secret I think you knew: I read the notebooks. I read them while you were sleeping in the truck or when you were out gathering firewood in some national forest I've since forgotten or when you drove into some nearby Lewisville or Clarksburg to get supplies. I think you wanted me to read them. That's why you left them around. I think you wanted me to read them so there would be at least one other person who knew what you felt. I think you wanted me to read them so I would know the things you wanted to do for me but were too good of a person to ask for. So I read the notebooks, then found a way to offer you those things without ever talking about it.

That was one of the games we played, wasn't it?

Drips and drabs of the notebooks showed up in magazines, always out of context so as to make you look like some kind of big pervert. There is even a manuscript on the internet that's supposed to be your journal but is really just a pisspoor retread of the Marquis de Sade mixed with a little triple A travel guide commentary.

But, then again, maybe you really were a big pervert, *and so am I!*

But I'll just pretend I'm not. I'll assume I'm not. I'll just continue thinking — rightly or wrongly — that all women, in their heart of hearts, if they are *really* honest with themselves, would give their eyeteeth to have a man the way I had you.

So every day now I sit at a table and I try to recreate your notebooks in my mind. Then I started filling in the conversations around the writing. You know. The things we talked about when we were around the campfire or driving down the road. Then I add what you must have been thinking.

I realize now how worried you must have been while you told me those protective lies I was so willing to believe.

I'm sorry. That's a big part of what I'm saying now. I'm sorry. There were any number of times along the line when I could have stopped things before they got so far out of hand. I was foolish and you loved me anyway. You never held me responsible for anything.

I'm sorry.

I'm so sorry.

I CHANGED THE story around a lot. Left some things out and made other things up. Not important things but just enough small things so that I could tell myself that the story wasn't really about us whenever I needed to. I changed our names for instance. I changed the setting of some of the things we did too. I put Illinois in Iowa and Iowa in Indiana. I made an F-150 into a Silverado and a blue room into a white one. I made these changes and I could write about the other things that really mattered. It was just a question of how to say it.

WHEN THEY DRAGGED me back to Kentucky, they put you on trial. Not a trial in the courts, mind you, but in the whorehouse of public opinion. Television commentators and editorial page pimps held a fire sale. They just had to draw some *mor*-al, some con-*clu*-sion, some *rea*-son for what we did. So these great minds pondered and pondered and consulted psychiatrists and professors and lawyers and men of the cloth, and they all came up with the same verdict.

They blamed you.

You wore the pants. You were the boss. You were the one with all the power in the relationship.

Pretty funny, huh? You must have looked down from heaven and just laughed your ass off at those stodgy old shits who huffed and puffed and decried the *kinkiness* of it all while completely missing the Numero Uno Kink.

THEN WE COME to the end.

The end is there, of course, and I'm writing my way to it. I don't know how I'll handle it yet, but I know I'll deal with it some way; and I wonder, when I finish, if that will exorcise your ghost and free me from your memory. I wonder if I even want that to happen.

I wish I'd never met you.

If there had been no beginning there would be no end.

But I don't have to think about that yet. I'm thousands of words from the final chapter. For a while, I can still take refuge in the middle ground of this Realm of the Unreal, this fictional land of prophetic sonnets and durable dreams that seem so close we can hardly fail to grasp them, where you still drive the back roads under the dark night of the Republic, and I still lay my head on your shoulder.

Your Lolita

D.B. Wells, 24, lives in Kentucky in as much anonymity as possible. Her stories have appeared in *New York Stories, Chelsea, Yemassee, Redbook, Cleveland Magazine, Art Times, New Letters, The Raven Chronicles, Northwest Florida Review, Big Muddy, Peregrine, Fugue* and *Stories from the Blue Moon Cafe.* She is currently at work on her first novel.

To support herself, she dances.